# The End
# of All Things
# Planned For

CHRISTOPHER
PATRICK
STEFFEN

This is a work of fiction. It is not real. If this resembles any actual events, locales, or persons, living or dead; it's a coincidence. Get over it.

ISBN: 0985909129
ISBN-13: 978-0985909123

*for my twenties*

Dozens of sirens
humming with she's gone.
This is occupation. This is an air-raid.
This is starting over. This is the end of
all things planned for.

—Curtis Jensen/Form of Rocket, "This Is Occupation"

# ACKNOWLEDGMENTS

This book could not have been completed without very exacting help by Erik Lopez. He attempted to teach me how to revise. I am grateful. Michael Steffen, Jasna Filipovic, and Turi Fesler were important readers. For everyone who read pieces and incarnations in the early years, I am grateful as well. Thank you.

## BLAKE (SEPTEMBER 18, 2005)

We sit in the back corner booth of the Urban Lounge. It's a slow Sunday night, and the touring band that was supposed to headline had car trouble outside of Evanston. The local bands kept their pre-cancellation schedule and now it's only midnight with maybe fourteen people in the bar and filler records playing indie rock.

"I added a new character," says Nate. He throws his eyebrows up as he raises his stein to his mouth.

"I don't feel like I even know the only two characters I have so far," I say. I tap the table lightly with my middle fingernail quickly in double time.

"No, no, no. You're going about it all wrong. The idea is to never know the characters. They just do their thing and exit stage left." He puts his stein down and points to me as he says, "This new character is a love interest. Junay. Tom has just had sex with her and is lying in bed next to her freaked out by this huge railroad-track of a scar running across her stomach. Junay had a c-section before, but the child was still born. Get it?"

"Is that a joke you are *saying* to me, or do you use that

in your writing?"

Nate winks and says, "So cuddled up next to Junay, Tom is starting to freak out, because the whole time they were having sex he was thinking about the scar, like maybe it was a weak seam and she might just bust right open. A part of him is a little pissed off that she never told him she had the scar, let alone had had a baby which might not have been his business yet...but a gigantic, crooked, Raggedy-Ann smile of a scar was his business. Not to mention the fact that this scar made coitus run long (satisfactorily for her, uncomfortably for him). He was disgustingly curious about whether it would feel like a piece of taut yarn under his fingertips. And that's when I go into this sweet dream sequence."

"Dream sequences are always perfect to allow the writer the freedom to have imagination," I say and drink some beer.

"Shut up. As he's falling asleep, he begins to think that the scar is talking to him in one of those cartoon-talking-tree-trunk voices, and it tells him to come inside. In his dream his curiosity gets the best of him, and he ends climbing inside her womb, which is naturally decked out in red sofas and pillows like *I Dream of Jeannie's* bottle. In Junay's womb the umbilical cord is sitting in the corner tied in a knot, but also looks like the earpiece end of a telephone pre-rotary style. Tom realizes he can unknot the telephone and call God...."

# BLAKE (SEPTEMBER 21, 2002)

The speakers scream the end of a Megadeath song, Nate cuts his path through an unfamiliar neighborhood full of small houses with yards with undefined edges and no sidewalks. These houses have carried generations of families. Young couples with a child or two that they will carry through the school years. Some children leave home early. Some follow their parents into the next home.

I was a smart child at one time. A precocious youth. Perhaps a little too precautious.

On the main drag of fifty-fifth Nate comes down the hill and steers the Jeep into the Food 4 Less parking lot. He speeds along knocking the Jeep against the speed bumps, which fortunately are small, but still cause a full-frame rattling. I imagine many small nuts and bolts showering into our wake as if we're trying to bait a wild robot beast. Nate throws the Jeep in park over two stalls near the entrance.

"Let's hope the only handicapped person coming here this late is on a motorcycle."

"What?" asks Nate.

3

We walk inside the warehouse of a grocery store, amidst fifteen foot scaffolding shelves and palette-piled goods. Food 4 Less has minimal staffing, primarily a checker or two and some stockers, so this affords them to stay open twenty-four hours. When you're drunk, broke, and hungry you track places like this down. Luckily, this store is only a few back roads from Nate's condo. When we left the condo, Charly and the others were playing quarters with Keystone Light.

Stumbling through the candy aisle, Nate grabs a large bag of Twizzler Pull Aparts.

"This will stick your shits together so you don't have diarrhea," he says.

I am about to argue, but then I think why not? What do I know about the nutritional forces of sticking stools together? Maybe this is what concerns you when you live on your own. My kitchen always has some sort of food in it. Thank you, Mommie Dearest.

The trough of frozen dinners and pizzas seems almost limitless. Particularly when looking with drunk vision through dry contacts. I hunt for the perfect frozen pizza: something that balances my inebriation with my frugality.

"What the fuck are you doing?" asks Nate.

I look at him. I can feel my brow furrow. But then feeling my brow furled I realize I'm puzzled as to what he means. I'm standing here leaning over the frozen pizzas drawing across the frost on the cardboard box of a pepperoni pizza and humming. I'm humming.

"What, bro? You don't like music?"

"Do you know how fucking drunk you look doing that?"

"Because I am drunk," I say.

"Listen, dickhead, I don't want them calling the cops on us for drunk driving, because someone sees you weirding-out in the frozen food section."

"If you were a punk band, you would be the Buzzkills."

There is an explosion so loud that I immediately think the whole store has doubled over from a kidney punch. But it is a compound sound; the first sound (the loud report) is immediately paired with a piercing female scream. The immediate reaction is to run, but strangely I only think this and stand stock still. Nate sprints down the aisle, peers through one of the shelves in the direction of the gunshot, and then comes running back toward me waving his arms like he's fending off a beehive.

He passes me at a full sprint, so I race after him. When he gets to the end of the aisle, he somehow dives through the bottom shelf of the aisle along the wall in a smooth action-movie-style move. It looks so rad I almost distract myself and don't dare attempt the same thing. I climb through a hole that Nate made in the cereal boxes.

We're crouched in the narrow space between the shelf and the wall, and Nate says, "We've got to stay hidden."

"You can see right through these shelves. Plus, you took out like a bunch of cereal boxes when you dove." It's like this knowledge annoys Nate, and he vainly attempts to slide over so he can replace a few of the now crushed boxes of Post Raisin Bran at our feet.

"What the fuck's going on?" I ask.

"Two guys are robbing the front of the store."

"We've got to do something...ha, just kidding. Why would they rob a Food 4 Less? There can't possibly be more than a few thousand dollars in the till."

"Some people only need a few thousand dollars—"

"But it's armed robbery. The sentence is the same if they robbed this place or a jewelry store. Now that they've discharged a round it's even worse. Did they shoot someone?"

"No, that was the girl at the register. I think they're just trying to scare her."

"For what? She doesn't own the place. What the fuck does she care?" I ask.

"I don't know," Nate says. "Why are you asking *me* all of this?"

Past the endless frozen trough in front of us, a man in all black walks past with a slight swagger. He carries a shotgun with the butt tucked into his armpit like a southern gentleman; the barrel sways lazily in front of him. He passes our aisle and out of our sight to the right.

"What the fuck?" I whisper. Nate shrugs. "Slide down behind that dog food."

Nate turns to his left and then starts sidestepping along the wall. The dust is thick enough to leave dirty streaks across our shirts. I keep feeling the delicate teases of cobwebs brush against my cheek. There could be spiders back here. There are big doors and food, which means there are flies. It'd make sense that there are spiders.

"This sucks," I whisper to Nate, and he stops.

"I'm getting my shit ready to stash if they find us," he whispers.

"What?" I ask and watch him fumble with something in his left pocket.

"If they look for customers. *Pulp Fiction.* They might want our wallets. I'm stashing all of my money and cards here." He slides his stuff under the dog food bag in front of him.

The store is eerily quiet.

"Good call." I slide my wallet out and pull the cash and cards. I pause. "But what if they look in our wallets? Why would we come to a grocery store with no money?"

"We like to shoplift." Nate smiles and shrugs. "OK. Leave five dollars in your wallet."

"Why am I the one putting five dollars in my wallet? We should both put five dollars in our wallets."

Nate says fine and takes some money to put in his wallet.

"Did you use a five or ones?" I ask.

"A five."

"Good, I used ones."

We stand in silence for a few minutes. Neither the man with the gun nor any other customers cross the aisles. The store has become empty, all action frozen. It's peaceful, seductively so. I wonder if there is an exit in the back of the store we could slip out. Might not have to buy our pizzas.

I worry that the moment we step out from behind the aisle is the moment the gunman returns. It's better to be patient. Nate opens the package of Twizzler Pull Aparts and begins to eat. I look at him, and he shrugs. I take one.

"How long do you think we should stay back here?" he asks.

"I don't know. I keep thinking the cops will show up and that will be that."

"I wonder where in the Hell everyone else is? I know we weren't the only people here. We haven't seen one person walk by since the guy with the gun. You'd hear a scream or something if he was cutting everyone up."

"I wish we had a bag of Doritos or something."

"Good call. Chips would be nice."

We stand there longer and don't hear anything or see anyone. It's becoming almost ridiculous we haven't heard a siren or even a car speeding off. No other customers. The guy with the gun has not come back.

"Where is everybody?" I ask. I don't even whisper.

"It's a little annoying," says Nate, also not whispering.

"Let's go," I say and start sliding back to where the cereal is, because I've decided it will be easier to crawl through light cereal boxes than heavy bags of dog food. Nate grabs his cash and cards as well.

"Hold up. I just thought of something. If we go out there and there are cops, they're going to want to interview us. They'll be able to figure out that we're drunk, and they'll bust us, well me, for drunk driving."

"We'll just tell them we walked here."

"They'll run the plates of my Jeep to make sure that everyone in the store is accounted for."

"Maybe they aren't even here."

"That's a hell of a gamble for a little lack of patience," he says.

"Look, throw your phone on silent, and I'll go out there and call you with the situation. If someone is out there I'll tell them I walked here."

"What if the guy with the gun is out there?" he asks.

"I won't call you."

"Nice."

I crouch and slide through the shelf knocking over the cereal boxes I had replaced. I put them back on the shelf and brush the dust off me. There's no one to my right or left or down the aisle. I decide it's safer to walk to my left scaling along the side of the store rather than cutting into the center.

The store is silent and seemingly empty. I reach the front and walk steadily toward the door. I don't even turn back for fear of spoiling my solitude. The door slides open, a noise uncomfortably loud, and I step outside.

There is a twenty-year old beaten BMW crooked on the front curb, but other than that, everything appears normal. I walk over and sit in the passenger seat of Nate's

Jeep. I look around and see no one. A few cars drive by on the street, but appear oblivious to any abnormalities. I pull out my cell phone and call Nate.

"There is no one here. Like, no one in the whole store. I'm sitting in your Jeep in the parking lot and no one is here."

"Cool, I'm on my way."

"Hey...grab a pizza on the way."

"Golden," he says.

I sit there and wait in the quiet trying to figure out what in the hell happened. It occurs to me that maybe none of this happened, but then why is nobody in the store now? I become a bit twitchy waiting for Nate to appear.

After a minute, he walks outside casually carrying a grocery bag.

"Did you buy that?" I ask.

"No one was there," he says. "I stood at the register, but when no one came I put my food in a bag and left." He pulls the Jeep out of the parking spot and we drive away. The pizza isn't very good, because we cook it in the microwave.

# BLAKE (OCTOBER 13, 2005)

In the flurry of orders flooding into room service for the dinner rush, George Callahan thumbs the receipt-of-order lying on my table, runs his nail down the list, and then scurries around the corner to the kitchen line. The phone rings in the cashier's office, and every time it rings Sonja takes an order, and every time Sonja takes an order, the phone rings. I stretch cling wrap squares over the tops of two glasses of water and bring them over to the table for the order I'm building. George skips around the corner, his left hand balancing the two large, concave salad dishes, and his right hand carrying, with the aid of a napkin, two flat, searing pizza plates. I flip the hot box door under the table open for him. He sets the salads on top of the table and then kneels and slides the entrees into the box, careful not to touch the stainless steel of the box, now several hundred degrees, thanks to the burning sterno can. The pizzas placed securely, he whips his hand out of the box and says, "Jesus, Young B," kicking the box with his foot and waving his hand.

I smile at first, but the look on his face tells me he's

not joking.

"This one's ready to go, Y.B." he says. "The pizzas are in the hot box, and I've got the Caesar on this side," he points to the covered dish on the left side of the table, "and the mixed greens." He waves to the other dish. He's not telling me this because it matters. I won't have to remember this, because when I present the dishes to the guests in their room I will remove the covers. At that point it will be quite obvious which salad is which. George is pointing to these items, because he is mentally checking everything on the list. For years George worked in the film industry and the habit of double and triple checking lists has not escaped him. "Don't forget to knock quietly."

Hours later. If Van Gogh had roomed with Rimbaud rather than Gaugin. I ring the door bell to 1567 and then double knock on the heavily laquered, ornately routed door. I count to fifteen in my head while staring at the door with a smile. When the time is up I triple check my order and make sure I grabbed both a salt and pepper shaker. I hear some shuffling inside the room and a male voice says, "That the door?"

There is a pause.

The door opens to a Mediterranean woman with sharp eyes wearing a fluffy white robe. Her long hair is permed and her tan-smooth skin appears richer against the white of the robe.

She is striking enough that I miss a beat before saying, "Good evening, Ms. Hansen—"

"Come in." The normalcy of her voice is in utter contrast to her appearance. I follow the sway of her stride into the room. A man in his early thirties with a flattop sits on the couch with an absent grin.

"I thought you were the TV," he says.

I server-laugh and say, "That happens all the time Mr. Hansen. How is everything with the room, sir? How has everything been with the hotel?"

He sticks his arms out in a jerky movement like he wants to bear hug the entire room and then turns his head from side to side while nodding. "I. Cannot. Complain. This place is spectastic," he says and laughs to himself while looking at the woman. Her slight smile doesn't change. She doesn't say anything, but submissively sits on the couch next to Mr. Hansen and curls into his armpit.

"Spectastic. That's wonderful, sir," I say. I remove the glass coffee table and slide the room service table in front of them. I pull everything out of the hotbox and arrange all of their food for them, uncovering their dishes and removing the cling wrap from their drinks. When their places are set, everything aligned accordingly, I present their dishes to them in dining order. The woman doesn't blink and still looks at me with her ever-present smile. Mr. Hansen slightly bobs his head to everything I say.

"That looks excellent, buddy," he says as I hand him the bill presenter. He signs it and adds a tip with a dramatic gesture throwing a toothy-grin at the woman but she doesn't notice it. I walk out the door telling them to have a pleasant evening and encourage them to contact in-room dining if we can be of any further service.

*"Hasta lasagna,"* Mr. Hansen says. Walking down the hall I decide that there's only one way that couple's relationship works: it's purchased.

"I still think you should write a little short story that we can make into a movie," George Callahan says while helping me set an order. "My 8mm is ready to go." The enthusiasm and desperation with which he says this makes me feel awkward because it comes from the responsibility-free nature of someone who produces art for enjoyment. A decade older than me, I respect George, because he has spent his life pursuing his art.

"Yeah, it's something," I mumble.

"You still got to see some of the movies I made. I mean, they're not amazing or anything, but I got some great shots out in the Salt Flats and Slick Rock. I made a couple of shorts about two years ago with this one woman you really should meet. She's a writer. But we made some shorts from a couple of stories she wrote that went to some film festivals. Mostly silent stuff. We tried to tell the stories visually that she wrote."

I imagine George's 8mm silent films, active light engaged over textured surfaces, and try to envision a place where my stories fit. I want to explain to him that I'm not that type of writer. I don't have the necessary sense of mood or tone, but instead I keep nodding my head.

A little later, back in the table line, I double check my next order and complain to George Callahan about going all the way to 495, delivering a filet, and receiving no tip. I slice some bread when behind me I hear, "How d'you like me now, pa'tner?" and as I turn around, I take a handful of raspberries to the chest.

"What the fuck are you doing, Pedro?" He laughs and runs back behind the chef's fridges. Pedro is a hyper Guatemalan with an inability to interact with others without affecting a character. In many jobs this could be a problem, but for in-room dining it works well, because the entire time Pedro is with guests he affects a "servant character" with so much commitment guests believe that it is his real personality. With all of his different affectations, I wonder if he has a "real" personality.

I take the wet napkin from my back pocket and try to clean the beads of raspberry juice before they soak into my white coat and shirt. I bring some bread back to the table.

"Pedro's got to knock that shit off," I say.

"What happened?" asks Dirk. He waddles over to us carrying a bowl of soup to cling wrap. Dirk has the posture and stroll of someone whose parents never told him to straighten his back or walk with his toes forward.

"Pedro's on this gangster kick and threw a bunch of raspberries at me," I say.

"Why did he do that?" asks George.

"He just saw a gangster movie and thought it would be funny," says Dirk.

"He thinks he's a gangster now and wants to re-enact all of these scenes from the movie," I say. "For Christ's sake, he's twenty-four."

"I'll tell him to lay off the fruit," says George. Something about how George says it makes me think he has other things on his mind.

In the fourteenth floor hallway I see Pedro walking back.

"You got raspberry juice on my uniform, dick."

"Behold how good and how pleasant it is for brethren to dwell together in unity," he says. We walk toward the employee area and service elevators.

"Shut up," I say. "I don't see juice on your shirt."

"Walk with me," he says which we are already doing. "In 1099 when Jerusalem was captured by the Crusaders, there was an increase in the amount of pilgrims every year. The problem was that, though the infidels were driven out of the city, they still inhabited the surrounding mountain areas. Nine noble knights, who had distinguished themselves at the siege of Jerusalem, united in a brotherhood...."

I push my train of dirty dishes down the seventeenth floor hallway. The trick is to avoid running the tables into the wall when cornering and be careful the tablecloths don't catch under the wheels. Down the hall I see the vague outline of a housekeeper. It's too late at night for me to see that far. My contacts feel like stamps stuck to my eyeballs.

The housekeeper looks up from her cart. I think she recognizes me.

"Hey, there," says a familiar voice. It's Irene.

Her hair runs straight slightly past her shoulders a shade darker than I remember. She has soft red highlights that look like the searing rips in a black heart that's begun to beat red again. She has the complexion of a girl with auburn hair, usually not my style, but Irene pulls it off. I should have been able to recognize her standing taller than most housekeepers, who are squat immigrant mothers. I still have no idea why Irene works here. She should be running the counter at a gym or selling clothes at a vintage store.

"Why are you still here?" I ask. "I thought you guys got off at like nine-thirty."

"What...you don't want to see me?"

"Um...no, I just meant. Anyway, what are you up to tonight?" I ask.

"Why do you care; are you asking me out?"

"I don't ask girls out," I say. She raises her eyebrow. "I've got a girlfriend. Some of us are heading over to The Bayou. My friend, Nate, is meeting us. You should come, if you want." I shrug.

She smiles and then pushes her cart away. "We'll see," I hear her say down the hall.

At The Bayou I tip back my pilsner glass and finish the last of my beer listening to Nate lecture about how much of my life is wasted every day as a faceless member of the proletariat. Dirk sits on the other side of me with a big grin on his face, but I doubt he can follow the intricacies of the argument. At the far end of the table George Callahan is raptly conversing with our waitress, Caroline, about, what sounds like, the best elementary school to send children. I have listened to George talk about Caroline in room service before, and I wonder if his interest in her opinion is purely ideological.

Back to my right, Nate says, "Impossible. I'm sorry. There may be men and women far greater than you and me who can manage full-time jobs with full-time artistic pursuits, but we are not these people. Without a lifestyle conducive to our creative processes, we will never fulfill ourselves or *do* what it is we were meant to do." He says this last part and raises his glass to toast himself as punctuation to his thought.

A part of me understands what he is saying. Nate works ten hours a week filing for a law firm. When we each started writing novels just over a month ago, Nate took off like wildfire, cashing in on his free time. Slowly, I started building a bit of my own momentum. And then I woke up this morning and discovered that Annette deleted my entire manuscript before she left to Hawaii.

"Now is the time to be youthful, and blissfully carefree with regard to careers, to jobs, to responsibility. Now is your chance to take some time and get that novel back," Nate says trying to catch me eye-to-eye. Earlier today I called Nate in a panic. There wasn't anything for him to say, so I went to work. I think he is trying to say more now.

"As much as I would love to take the time, there is no way I can keep my apartment AND quit my job," I say. "Not going to happen."

"I don't think you need to quit your job," Dirk says. "My buddy, Shawn, works as an auto mechanic during the day, but then builds all of these sculptures once he is off. He even made a piece for that new park they are building in West Valley. The city is going to pay him five thousand dollars for it."

"That may work for your friend," says Nate, "but I don't think Blake is going to pony up every evening or every morning and step up to the plate himself. He's a bit of bitch that way."

"Fuck you. I had a hundred pages going. I was making things happen. What have you done that is so great?" I ask.

"I added this story to my novel about a guy named Mannie and a robot," Nate says.

"Mannie is a good name," I say.

"Precisely. The basic premise is that there is Mannie and his robot, Cheri. They are lovers. But Cheri doesn't look like a human. She looks like the kind of robot you'd see on *The Jetsons* or something. But she's totally human-like otherwise and sincere and fickle and feisty and everything else that girls or women are. Mannie and her are in love, and they can have sex, because she has this attachment thing that he puts over his junk and these electrodes he attaches and she can totally get him off. Like she can give him the best orgasms he's ever had, because she directly stimulates him. But he can't ever caress her or anything, because she's a big bulky robot. So the story goes that he starts having an affair with this human girl, Jill, that he meets at work. Jill is not really that attractive by human standards. She is kind of chunky and doesn't really do anything hot with her hair. Cheri finds out and gets super mad at Mannie and can't understand why he would cheat with someone who isn't very smart or doesn't really have a sense of humor. And he agrees and feels like a shit, but he is helpless to the temptation of human flesh. He can't not be turned on by her. And Cheri argues, 'But she's ugly.' And he says, 'But she's human.' And that's the crescendo. That's about how far I got, all while you were at work."

Dirk laughs and says, "I totally missed something there."

"How in the hell is that even part of a novel?" I ask.

Nate smiles and shrugs. "That's not the point. The point is your baby stepping," says Nate. "Now that you're back to scratch, you need to make up for lost time; otherwise, you'll never get the damn thing done."

"I love how much you care whether he writes," says Dirk. "You're like Y.B.'s life coach or something."

Nate says, "He's my boy. But I also think our projects are intrinsically linked. If Blake washes by the wayside, I know that I will never complete what I am doing either. It's weird that you can rely on others for things like that, but Blake got me off of my ass, and now it is my job to keep him off of his."

"I don't get why Annette deleted your book," says Dirk. "Is she just a bitch or something?"

Nate smirks, but I say, "In my book the main character started falling in love with a co-worker. My guess is that Annette read that and thought it was real."

Caroline sets another two pitchers on our table. I didn't even notice that she and George had broken conversation, but it occurs to me that George has probably spent the last five minutes mutely staring around the bar checking women out. Something about him seems off. I want to ask him what is up, but I can't while we are all sitting here.

We fill all of our glasses and raise them in cheers before taking healthy gulps. Dirk reaches up and points to the front door of the bar.

"Isn't that Irene?" he asks.

Irene has big loopy earrings, and her hair pulled back in a ponytail. The doorman looks at her ID and says something to her. She points in our direction and George waves so the doorman lets her enter without having to buy a club membership.

When she walks over to us, George says, "Irene, come and join us. Have a seat."

"Thanks. Blake told me you guys were coming here." She looks at me and smiles. I smile back.

Nate turns toward me, away from Irene, and raises his eyebrow. I shrug in response, while Irene talks to George. For the next two hours, we drink and talk. We ask Irene about school and she tells us about studying art. She tells us that she may try to get into law school. Nate tells her about the novels he and I are writing. He tells her that I have to start over from scratch, because of my girlfriend. At one point he begins to imply that I should break up with Annette, but I cut him off.

By the end of the night I'm tired. Talking is an effort, and I'm afraid I will become belligerent. I follow Nate to the bathroom and realize how difficult walking is. The people I pass on the way to the bathroom sway, and I don't think my contact lenses work well. I wonder why I always have to pass pool tables on the way to the bathroom. My bladder hurts. The bathroom consists of a stall and a urinal. Nate takes the urinal.

"So what's your plan, *cap-ee-tan?"* Nate asks.

"What do you mean?"

"For after here."

"What do you think of Irene?" I ask.

"She reminds me of Annette. When I first saw her walk in the resemblance was uncanny."

"Jesus, you think? I never even thought about that."

"So?" Nate asks. I don't answer him, because we both know that I will go home alone. Whatever madness Annette and I are experiencing, it isn't officially over, so I won't complicate it. We wash our hands and walk back out to the table. Everyone is itchy to leave and shuffling coats back and forth.

# BLAKE (OCTOBER 11, 2002)

I tap my thigh as I walk through the video store and look at all of the annoying couples trace the New Releases wall. The only people not part of a couple are the teenagers who do the same thing but stay in packs. I walk through the Foreign section and decide that I am the only *individual* in this place when I see a lonely, heavy woman with short curly hair, probably in her mid-thirties, slowly scanning the Drama section. The woman senses that she is being watched and starts to look in my direction so I quickly avert my gaze and grab a Japanese horror movie about a little girl with black eyes. The movie looks terrible, and I put it back.

Nate and the condo kids are in Wendover all weekend. They asked me to come, but I decided against it, because when they described the trip it sounded like one prolonged expense. This evening Taylor had already taken off with one of his friends before I got home from work, so I sat in the basement alone watching TV and then decided I was going to lose my mind. For lack of any place else to go, I decided to rent a couple of movies.

The camaraderie of everyone in the video store bugs me. All of the guys sound like loud assholes and everything they say sounds pedestrian and boring. "Dude, Jodie Foster is *hot* in that one." "The cars in that movie are awesome." In my desperation to leave I grab some French movie about a woman whose whole family dies in a car accident.

At the cash register I stand behind a woman who keeps asking for information about an eight dollar late fee.

"When was this? When were the movies rented?" the woman asks.

The girl at the counter looks at her computer screen and says, "Both movies were rented on September 26th."

"September 26th?" The woman leans against the counter and cranes her head to try and see the girl's computer screen. "That doesn't sound right. I don't remember renting anything then. What movies were they...."

The woman does not have to be dealing with this right now. When she first approached the counter and handed her membership card, the girl merely asked if the woman would *like* to pay her late fees at this time. The girl was not requiring the woman to do this, but the woman, in defiance of any sort of long-line etiquette, turned the question into a five minute discussion. I can tell that I am not the only anxious one, because the couples in line behind me aren't talking and even the three teenage boys are quiet.

The woman does not pay her late fees, but pays for her current rentals and leaves. I approach the counter and slide my movies and membership card over to the girl. Now really looking at her, I realize that not only is she hot, but I know her from a short story workshop I had.

She scans my membership and then pauses for a minute and turns back to me with a smile that erases all of her frustration from the previous customer. "Blake?" she asks. "Blake Matts?"

"How are you?" I reply.

"It's Annette. From Dr. Lambert's workshop." Annette's eyes glow in excitement.

"I know," I say. "You still in school?"

Annette slides the movies under the scanner and says, "I have another year. You graduate?"

"I did," I say. "I have a fancy office job…no, I'm kidding. I work at this office, and I'm going to quit. It's horrible."

Annette takes the movies over to the exit, and I step around the corner of the counter. She wishes me luck with finding a job and tells me it is good to see me again. I tell her that I will come back and rent more movies soon. Once I am home I call the store, and I ask her out. We exchange phone numbers and make plans to talk in a couple of days.

# TAYLOR (SEPTEMBER 23, 2005)

In class Dr. Johnson cycles around our easels following the progress of our still lifes. Dr. Johnson always sports an over-sized overcoat cinched around the waist and pants too large for his five-foot-six frame. His hair is bushy and grey and ages him well past the smooth skin of his face. He struts among the different easels pointing at various colors and asks the students if they think that the orange should be warm, if the green should be opaque. Along the side of the classroom three direct sources light the subject, which are a jar of peppers (one red, the rest green), a dark red raincoat, and a porcelain kabuki mask. These three objects sit on an orange table half-covered by a green afghan. The students randomly station around these objects. Like every classroom in the Art and Architecture Building, this one is cavernous with grey windows and fifteen-foot concrete ceilings.

So far I've set the ground color and painted the afghan and table. I feel like my initial tones are too warm for the piece, but I am too anxious to repaint them. By adjusting my palette's overall tone I hope to compensate.

While mixing some cadmium red and yellow to start the jar, I struggle capturing the transparency of the glass's effect on the peppers. The way the light shines on them and the effect of the gleam. When I add the yellow the color becomes too warm, and when I try to compensate with some lemon yellow the color becomes too light.

Dr. Johnson finally makes his way to my easel and asks, "You imagine these objects set in a grassy meadow on a summer day, I suppose?"

"I imagine the objects and I sipping a shiraz on a picnic. Red and white checkered cloth," I say. Dr. Johnson smiles at me. "My colors are a bit warm, but I'm going to balance that with cooler objects. I don't want to have to redo my ground at this point. The contrasts will make everything more intense."

"More intense or out of balance? It might be worth questioning, is the ground less important than the subject? Would the Parthenon still be standing if the foundation were sandstone?"

I stare at him and don't say anything. He breaks his smile.

"At this point it *isn't* worth starting over again," he says. "But next week when we start a new piece, I want you to concentrate more on your ground. You've got the technique down, but your colors are still loose."

I mumble OK as he glides to the next student. Part of me admires Dr. Johnson in the classroom. He's very inspirational when he lectures. The other part of me remembers that he's a failed artist. Never will produce a lasting work. And I don't blame the medium, he just doesn't have it in him.

To my right, Carrie has set a good ground, balanced the table and afghan, and finished the raincoat. She stands away from the work checking her scale.

"That looks good," I say. "Did you come in last night?"

"No," she says, "but I stayed later on Monday. What are you working on now?"

"I'm going to start with the jar, but I'm having color trouble. I'll probably stay after today. Probably have to."

"I like staying later," she says. "If I could stay today I would. It's nice painting when no one else is here."

Carrie is a stocky girl who will become a professional artist one day. She throws herself into her work with an admirable dedication. She lives and breathes for her art and is one of three people whose opinion I pay attention to during critiques.

An hour and a half pass during which most of the class leaves. Martin and Lacy are the only students still painting. I am still looking at the same damn coat, mask, and peppers and still going half blind staring at the colors. The clock is ticking, and I will have to leave soon to go to work. Eighty percent of the class finished by the end of class time, and I don't understand why it takes me so much longer.

I skipped the peppers and painted the coat. I'm finishing the mask although not entirely satisfied with its shape. In my painting the mask appears to be smiling rather than frowning. I haven't painted the lines wrong but the initial shape was off so the perspective is killing me. It's like the painting is laughing at me. Now the colors and the perspective are a problem. For a minute I'm tempted to throw my painting across the room. The mocking laugh. I want to stab right through my mask. I want to tear the piece of canvas out and burn it.

But I sigh. Fuck it. I just want the painting to be over. As soon as it's graded, I'll immediately gesso over the entire canvas.

I sit on a stool behind me and stare at the subject.

Martin says, "Not going well." Martin's brilliant perception is reflected in his terrible paintings.

"I fucking hate painting this crap," I say.

"I know what you mean. Much more of this and I'd become a photography student."

"This stuff sucks for me, because my red-green vision isn't even very good to begin with. Like on those tests with the pink bubbles, I can't even see whatever it is one is supposed to see. That's like all this is."

"That would suck," he says.

Yeah. I stand up and try to mix the colors for the peppers. I'm running low on palette space, but somehow I nail the colors. I paint the peppers in the jar. The red pepper is last and should be easiest. Murphy's law is making my skin creep, and my hand isn't as steady. When I get the color, I paint it on and twitch one stroke. The twitch puts a mark over a green pepper. I switch brushes and try to go over the red mark, but it darkens the entire pepper. Now I have some green peppers, a red pepper, and a brown pepper. I can't lighten the one pepper and don't want to have to repaint the jar. I'll have to clean my palette off and start from scratch.

I pick up the painting and walk out of the room, banging the corner of my painting against the doorway. I walk down one of the building's cavernous halls. When my painting slips, I let it drag along the concrete floor. I take the slow elevator down from the third floor to the first. I drag my painting to the entrance and slam it through the doorway.

Once outside I run and throw my painting into the tree branches. The Art and Architecture Building sits on a hill, but has flat lawn areas that head out horizontally before dropping twenty feet to the parking lot. A flight of stairs bisects the two lawn areas and leads to the parking lot.

My painting hits the trunk of the tree and then crashes through various branches, brushing over twigs as it makes its way down the twenty feet. I walk to the railing along the edge of the lawn area and look down to see my painting, face down in the dirt. In the parking lot a couple students standing next to a truck laugh. I wave. The sky is grey, and in a couple of months it will start to snow. I debate whether or not to repaint the jar of peppers.

# BLAKE (OCTOBER 14, 2002)

I sit in the family room with my father watching *First Blood*.

"I'm supposed to be going out," I say. "This girl I had a workshop with a year ago. Ran into her at the video store. She's supposed to call me back." My father looks from me back to the TV.

An hour passes with Rambo still being chased, and I keep looking at my phone which tells me the time and that I have not received any phone calls. I pull my phone out again and flip it open, and my father looks at me like I'm a sad clown. I don't need his pity, and I focus on the movie.

When the phone finally rings I run it down to the basement before answering.

"Sorry, I should have called you sooner. I was talking to my friend Amy. She's losing her mind over this long report she has to write for her rhetoric class," Annette says all of this in one breath.

"Crazy," I say. "I just watched *First Blood* with my dad."

"Great, how was that?" Annette asks.

"It was Rambo," I say. "What did you want to do this evening? I know a band that is playing at the Urban Lounge."

"It's a bar, isn't it? I'm not twenty-one. We could go bowling or go to a movie," she says.

Both of these options sound like stupid wastes of money to me, but I tell her that they are great ideas. She asks if I can come to her parents' townhome and tells me to bring some alcohol. I write down the address.

In my room I have the bottom third of a fifth of vodka, half of a cherry wine cooler, and a finger of Everclear. I mix it all together in the vodka bottle and shake it up. The drink is bright red and smells like sweetened gasoline. I stick the bottle in my backpack.

I drive over to the address and enter a brand new gated community. Annette's parents' townhome is half of the first duplex inside the gate next to what looks like two or three empty lots. The other side of the street is more developed. The porch light shines from the otherwise dark townhome.

Annette lets me into a dark foyer and tells me that her parents are living in Nebraska right now. They keep the townhome for when they want to come out and visit her and her sister. The floors are hardwood, and the kitchen appliances are stainless steel as well as the refrigerator. Opposite the kitchen, at the far end of an over-sized, unfinished wooden dinner table is a stonework and marble gas fireplace.

"This is a nice place," I say.

"Thanks," she says. "Did you bring any alcohol?"

I open my backpack and set the vodka bottle on the counter in her kitchen. "That is a special Blake Matts mix. It's not fantastic," I say, "but it will get you drunk."

She takes a couple of glasses from the cupboard next to the sink and pours us glassfuls. I raise my glass in a toast and take a drink trying not to wince.

"How is it?" she asks.

"It's...fire," I say and gasp.

"You can't even pretend that it tastes good," Annette says.

She laughs and then tries to chug her entire glass. The second she removes the glass from her face, I can tell that bad things are about to happen. Immediately she runs over to the sink and begins vomiting. Because of the color of the alcohol, she appears to be vomiting blood. I try to help by holding her hair.

When her stomach settles I walk her over to a couch with her arm over my shoulders. I doubt she needs this much help, but it gets me close to her. She lies on the couch, and I put her feet up and then go and get a glass of water. I kneel down next to her and tell her to drink some water. Her mouth and lips are red from the drink and she looks like a little girl who has tried to apply her mom's lipstick.

"I'm sorry," she says. "I guess I ruined the night."

"You're fine. Don't worry about it," I say and brush her bangs with my fingers. I lean over her. When my face is close enough, I rub my lips on her cheek. She lets me kiss her. After a few minutes of kissing on the couch, she asks if I want to go upstairs. It's one of those questions....

We make out in her parents' bed, and when I go to slide my hand down her pants, she moans and says, "Stick it in."

I mumble, "What me...or my hand," but Annette doesn't hear me. We make love terribly and at one point she looks at my face and asks me if I'm OK. The next day I email her a very sweet email that leads to our second date.

# BLAKE (OCTOBER 14, 2005)

Pedro, Dirk, and I each cram a table into the elevator. There's a mini-rush from the arriving conference group. My order is two Kids meals for a single diner: a macaroni and cheese and a Kids burger. Guests who want to save money order Kids meals. Cheap guests. As the elevator begins to rise, I bump my table and the little porcelain vase and rose tip off. The vase breaks into several pieces, which I gather up quickly. Dirk says, "You shouldn't do that with your hands," and I notice the line of blood appear along the side of my index finger.

"I don't want to have to go back for a flower," I say. Now the table is missing its rose and my hand is bleeding. If I go back downstairs for another rose and a bandage, this order and the following three will all be late.

The elevator opens and Dirk pushes his table out, "Fuck it. They're poor; they don't give a shit about a flower." The elevator closes.

I think back an hour to when Theodore, our Brazilian manager replete with braids pulled back into a ponytail, made us do a line-up like in-room dining was a real restaurant. He proceeded to tell us about the First Step Organization. Eighty percent of the hotel was booked by this non-profit group whose mission was primarily social work (something with getting single mothers and troubled individuals jobs). The opportunity to stay in a five-star hotel for a week for free was the reward for hours of low-pay labor. "These types are not the usual crowd we get here. They don't have money," Theodore said.

"That's kind of fucked up," said George Callahan, "that these people with no money are left here to fend for themselves when they can't afford to eat here."

"We're not going to make shit in tips," said Pedro. Theodore responded by shaking his head and shrugging.

Back in the elevator I take the cloth napkin from my back pocket and wrap it around my finger. "I guess I could hold this over my finger," I tell Pedro in the elevator. I attempt to readjust it to conceal any bloodspots.

Pedro looks at me like I'm crazy, but there's no way I'm going back downstairs for someone who's not even tipping. I just hope the damn thing doesn't fall off. I push my table out of the elevator on the eighteenth floor. Pedro wishes me luck.

I pause in front of the door.

Five minutes from now when I'm in the elevator going downstairs. I ring the bell. From behind the door someone says just a minute and then opens it.

"Good afternoon, Ms. Harvey. May I come in?" I push the table into the room without waiting for a response.

Ms. Harvey appears to be in her forties, but has the sun-hardened wrinkles of a river guide. She wears acid-wash jeans and a turquoise t-shirt advertising Jed's Crab Shack. Her ratty hair falls short of shoulder-length with two inches of natural brown hair growing out of her scalp and the rest a dyed straw-blond. Behind her thick glasses, she has kind eyes.

"I've never stayed at a hotel that has a doorbell," she says.

"It's kinda funny," I say. I start setting up her table without drawing attention to the napkin wrapped around my finger. "Has everything been OK with the room? Lights, TV?"

"Oh, are you kidding me? This room's amazing. I called my husband as soon as I arrived, and I told him, you'll never believe this: I have a separate family room and bedroom with doors in-between. He got a kick out of that...."

I burn my knuckles on the inside of the hot box while attempting to put out the little burning can of sterno. Typically, I use my cloth napkin to pat out the flame, but with my finger wrapped in it, I had to swat at the flame with the bundle. I've got to get out of this room.

"...Right near Biloxi. A little bit north. We stay in those little motels on the beach occasionally, but never anything like this."

I present the Kids meals to her and ask for her signature. She hasn't noticed my finger and seems genuinely giddy about the whole experience until she reads the bill.

"Thirty dollars? I didn't know there is a delivery charge *and* a service charge."

"I'm sorry about that. I think it explains it on the bottom of the room service menu."

"Oh...I guess I'll have to ask the girl on the phone for the total in the future." The woman scribbles on the receipt, and I take the bill presenter from her.

"Sure, she'd be happy to tell you that." I leave her room nearly skipping back to the elevator.

# BLAKE (OCTOBER 15, 2005)

I listen to George Callahan tell Dirk how he's going to bring his sixteen millimeter out to the salt flats to shoot some sunsets for a film he is making. George drives his van with Dirk in the passenger seat. I sit in a rear seat with my arms draped over the back, because the seat doesn't have any visible seat belts. The back of the van is packed with camping equipment and a couple of large durable black cases that may have to do with George's camera equipment. A fine, earthy silt covers the equipment, and I keep swatting at my pants to remove the dust.

"There's a mini-fridge in the back next to Blake that I stock full of beer. This is the most amazing van for road trips. With some extra gas I could probably camp in this thing for two or three days. Get completely away from the city. It's the greatest feeling in the world. No cars, no electricity; you don't see anyone."

"Sounds a little like psycho-ville to me," says Dirk and laughs. "You aren't related to the Mansons or anything?"

I try to make a joke about not giving George my

mailing address, but it is lost in the noise of the drive. I ask a little louder, "Where is this party supposed to be?"

"I told you, it's in my old neighborhood," says Dirk. "My friend, Chet, is there."

"You don't have any friends," I say.

"I don't have to drive all the way to Magna do I?" asks George.

The last two shifts of work have been brutal. The women in the First Step Organization have no money and end up pooling what they have to pay for one entrée. There are no tips and many of the guests pay in change, because they don't have room credit to sign for food.

Right after work Dirk stole a bottle of Jack Daniels, and the three of us hid in the stairway between the internal guest parking lot and the street, drinking. The stairway was made up of cement stairs with thick white paint on the steel handrails and cinderblock walls. All employee areas of the Grand National Hotel are thoroughly lacquered in white paint. The hotel employs a full-time staff specifically for the painting and repainting of every wall, handrail, and door. The cold air in the stairway carried the remnants of an infinite number of smoking employees passing through the stairway on their way out of the hotel. We sat one flight of stairs above any employee traffic and passed the bottle back and forth.

"I've got the entire order set up and ready to serve on the table and the guy asks me if I can move the coffee table back and transfer everything to it," said Dirk.

"That sucks," I said.

"So I tell the guy, it's not all going to fit on the coffee table, but he has me do it anyway. Then once everything is moved over, and I have to stack everything on top of everything else just so it will fit, he smirks at me like, told you so. I ask if he wants me to leave the room service table, and he says no, and then he doesn't even tip me. I mean come on, man, I'm in your room for practically ten minutes moving everything around for you."

"I figured you were probably taking a smoke break," said George Callahan. He passed the bottle to Dirk who took a solid pull.

"I could have in the time I was up in that room."

"Do you think they have any cameras in here?" I asked.

"Do you see any cameras?" asked Dirk.

"With my contacts, I can't see anything."

"They have a camera on the outside of the building that looks at the door and street corner, and they have a camera inside the guest parking lot that can be turned to see the other door of the stairway," said George.

"I'm sketched sitting here. It's like the perfect reason to get fired. I don't need that right now. I'm already losing my girlfriend," I said.

"Take a shot, Young B." said George. Dirk passed me the bottle. George asked, "I thought you were going to call Annette in Hawaii?"

I took a hard pull, gulping twice, and coughed.

"There it is," said Dirk. "George let me use your cell phone. I'll see if I can find us a party to go to." Dirk put the phone to his ear and turned to me, "I thought you were working out something with that housekeeper?"

Dirk reached a friend of his that told him about a party, and George offered to drive. I went with them, because I didn't want to get a D.U.I. driving home.


Annette has been gone for three days. I still haven't called her.

"What the fuck kind of party is this, though?"

"It's a kegger," says Dirk.

"Are these like friends, or thug friends, or this a dealer you know or something?" I ask.

"This is one of my oldest friends, from when I first lived in Utah when I was fifteen. Chet's a cool kid. He lives with like four guys. They rent a house."

"Is there going to be some tight pussy at this party?" asks George.

"If there was, you wouldn't be getting any of it...no, I'm kidding. Actually, it's a party full of homosexuals, George. You should fit right in."

"I just better not be driving all the way out to Magna," says George.

After twenty minutes of listening to the oldies we're down the street from a house with few neighbors. In the dark it is hard to verify, but the neighborhood appears to consist of houses situated in the middle of large lots for pastureland. I can smell the manure. The street is lined with cars on both sides.

George Callahan looks down the stretch of cars in front of him. "This is a good sign, fellas. Dirk might not be talking out of his ass after all."

We walk down the sidewalk toward the house. The door to the house swings open and a boy in his late teens goes running out of the house with a plastic cup in his hand. He's wearing black pants, a white shirt, and black tie. He wears a navy sport coat with his sleeves pushed to his elbows. He runs into the street as a girl about the same age chases after him in a sparkly dress. She's barefoot. She screams, "Michael," and throws the beer in her cup into the street. The boy stops half a block away, laughing. The girl begins walking toward him, but we walk in the door before I find out what happens.

Inside the house a group of high-school-aged kids look up to us from their couches in the front room. We interrupt their discussion about their friends that have just gone running out of the house. George says hi, but the three of us walk past the room before they respond.

In the kitchen two men in their early twenties sit on stools around the counter. They have a stack of blue plastic Dixie cups in front of them.

"Good evening, gentlemen. Can we help you?" asks the one on the left. He wears an orange t-shirt and has short, highlighted hair that is gelled into little spikes and hoops in both of his ears.

"My friend Chet called me from here," Dirk says.

"You one of Chet's friends?" the one on the left says. "I'm Steve and this is Buck..." he introduces his large friend on the stool to his left. Buck wears jeans and a jean-jacket and juts a toothpick out of his lower lip. He waves a hand.

Dirk introduces us and says nice party.

"Most everyone is out back in the barn," says Steve. "Cups are five dollars."

"What kind of beer is it?" asks George. "Can you get me, Dirk? I'll give you cash tomorrow."

"I don't roll with cash," says Dirk. But he pulls out a ten, and I give Steve a five.

"Enjoy yourselves," says Steve.

In the backyard there are scatterings of conversation coming from the assorted small groups. Little cigarette ends glow and buzz around. I can make out the barn about twenty yards away. Loud music and strobe lights leak out the walls. Dirk pulls a cigarette out of his pocket and lights up.

"Any of you guys want a pull? It's a sneaky toke," he says waving the little plastic joint toward us.

"I'll try some," says George Callahan. He pulls the joint toward his mouth. "Do I have to hold a lighter to it while I'm inhaling?"

"It's already cherry," says Dirk.

George Callahan begins coughing at the peak of his inhale. He coughs loudly and painfully and I sense people around us are watching.

"What about you?" he asks. George keeps coughing, but also laughs at himself.

"I'm going to stay on the alky wave," I say.

"Come on, Young B." says George Callahan.

"I paid five bucks," I say.

Dirk takes a hit and exhales his smoke in my face.

"Thank you," I say. He laughs.

We walk over to the barn. I stop in front of it, but Dirk pulls it open, and we walk in. Through the flashing lights people dance and huddle around the DJ's table in the corner. The music is some house techno, heavy-base thing full of synthetic melodies and pitches. The air is thick with sweat and moisture from a mist machine that irregularly sprays over the dancers. George Callahan pats me on the shoulder and cuts in front of us. Dirk and I follow him around the dance floor to a keg in the corner of the room across from the DJ. The line has about twenty people in it and moves slowly. We can't talk because of the music, but Dirk and I watch the dancers, and he throws me a bright look and nods his head. The girl dancing closest to us could be seventeen or twenty-two.

I've already begun bobbing my head to the beat. I'm still too sober to dance, but I want something from the rhythm. It takes a full twenty seconds to fill my cup with beer. I try in vain to pump the keg twice, but the beer won't come any faster. The keg is chilled in a large rubber garbage can filled with ice. I wait for Dirk and George Callahan to fill their cups, and then I walk to the back of the keg line. George and Dirk both smile at me, but nod their head away from the line. I point through the line toward the keg. They shrug and walk off.

In front of me in line a brunette in tight black pants and a halter top turns to me. I smile and raise my cup in tribute to her. She turns back to the keg. I stay through the keg line for three full refills, but then walk through a mass of people to find a bathroom. While following the wall I remember we're in a barn (ie. no plumbing) and amend my thinking. I make for the door.

My eyes are better adjusted to the night when I exit the barn. I can see three distinct clusters of people talking in between the house and the barn. Through the humming in my ears, I hear the bass pounding through the wooden walls of the barn. The yard stretches a good distance to both my right and left, and there are no bushes. I walk around the barn. A small group of guys turn to me when I round the corner. I say hello...and then walk back around to the side of the barn. I piss on the side of the barn, making the wood turn black, and try to stand close enough to the wall to conceal my activity while standing far enough away to avoid the misty splash.

My world is various shades of grey blues and black greens. Snippets of chatter mix with the beat pounding on the walls of the barn. My ears ring at different volumes. I want to find George Callahan and Dirk. I try the barn first.

Walking back into the barn is different. The atmosphere is palatable and tastes like mist and sugar candy. Every few seconds bright lights flash on different people in front of me and my head registers these nameless snapshots into an album. Two guys dressed off brand-name racks, with chewing gum and earrings smile at each other. A girl, back pressed into the chest of one, holding the other to her hip, with both blond and black hair, throws her head back to release a little glowing angel from her tongue. Her red nails squeeze into his sleeves in that instant. Two guys with beer cups synchronously look at me. One wears a necklace made from little shells. Around couches to the side of the dancing, I capture a group who obviously all know each other, and none know me. I focus on a couple just off the center. The girl sits cross-legged with her t-shirt pulled up exposing her back and sweaty torso. Her hair is matted to her head and gathered in a tight bun. A boyfriend or lover massages her back. He wears a painter's mask. In another glimpse, one of three guys is exhaling smoke in my face. My eyes cut right through the myrrh, and I imagine my cavalier, jaded look. My eyelids hang low. A hand is patting me on the back again. George Callahan guides me from the perimeter to the dance floor. He tries yelling into my ear, but I can't hear what he says. He leads me to a girl who is either in her late teens or early twenties. She has dark hair and dark eyes that crinkle in the corner with her smile, and she wears a tank-top that exposes her olive skin accompanied by a candy necklace. She tries to say something in my ear, but I shake my head. George has an arm around her, and they both respond by shrugging and leaving me.

I lose myself in the dance beat. With the heavy base, mist, melody loops, and strobe lights, I pop and roll far away from the desert. I lose my co-workers at a stranger-party, move past Nate and the condo kids, the deleted novel, the unholy hotel and siren, and even far above my Annie lying over the ocean. I accept that this might be the closest I get to Enlightenment. But I can't stop trying to share this with someone. There is a chubby brunette in front of me with the most alluring gyrations. I dance near her, but she ignores me. She won't look at my face. I don't know how long I dance near her trying to put out some vibe.

I move back into the oceanic dance crowd. I see George Callahan making out with the girl with the candy necklace. I gravitate toward a tall, stick-limbed blonde with dark lipstick and eye make-up. She dances away from me as I approach....

I'm back in the keg line with an empty cup when Dirk taps me on the shoulder.

I can hear him say, "SWALLOW THIS," and he puts something small in my hand.

I furrow my brow and give it back to him.

A strobe light catches his glowing teeth and makes his pupils shine darker. I refill my cup, and we make our way out the barn. There are more people in the backyard now.

"What the fuck was that pill?" I can't tell how loud my voice is because of my ringing ears.

"Just don't say I never offered to give you anything," he says.

I smile, because this doesn't make sense in any context of every conversation we've ever had. I'm laughing. He's to the point where he can only speak in clichés. Don't say I never offered to give you anything. I've never asked for anything. It doesn't make sense in my favorite way. Dirk smiles while I laugh.

"Where've you been?" I ask him.

"Hanging out with Chet's friends. They're in the house. Have you seen George?"

"Last time I saw him, he was making out with a girl that might have been half his age. He's on the dance floor."

"You're serious? I hope he doesn't want to go home

44

with her, or we're going to have to find another ride."

"Fuck that. What's his wife going to think?"

"She threw him out a couple of days ago," says Dirk. He pulls something out of his pocket and lights it. It smells like weed.

"He never told me that."

"He gave me a ride home from work the day it happened. He's staying with his parents."

"That is so lame. He never said anything." I feel like a prick now, but for no specific reason. Thirty-five years old and living with your parents. I wish Dirk was Nate. Why would George Callahan tell Dirk and not me? "I think I'm getting some more beer," I tell Dirk. He follows me inside. I want to be able to look through the crowd and see Annie. But maybe I already see her seeing me. And she's just out of my range of vision and I hate it. I hate me. I don't want to be thirty-five. In the middle of the dance floor a black man wearing some sort of priestly robe bangs the rhythm against a book. I might ask Dirk for that pill.

Ears full of static. Like climbing out a pool or coming down the mountain. It must be a basement, everyone in a circle, passing smoke around. I'm not following any of the conversations, and if Dirk weren't sitting next to me I'd have already gotten off the couch. All of these people are talking to other people. All of these conversations.

And to my right she says, "What do you think?"

These people must be in their early thirties. My mind feels like it is sharpening and everything is becoming incredibly vivid. There's a girl to my right asking me about Ethiopia. Dirk is talking to that Chet kid, and I think I shook his hand. I don't know where the girl came from or what her name is. There's a black guy in a robe across from us, and he was talking and that's what she was asking me about. And he looks so familiar. He's preaching to the people around him.

Chet falls off the couch, because he starts laughing when he leans too far forward. When Dirk goes to pick him up he can't, collapsing on top of Chet laughing. I don't think it's funny, but I laugh. Through my laughter I see the girl staring at me with a straight face. I can't even sit up straight. And everyone across from us stares and exhales smoke out his or her nostrils. I think about how much sense this makes. We are laughing too hard. We are the only ones fucked up. That's why they haven't cancelled their meeting.

George Callahan asks me why I'm sitting under a tree.

"This is a giving tree, G.C." He's holding the hand of some pretty girl in a tank-top I know from somewhere. "This is *the* giving tree."

"Blake, where's Dirk? Blake. Blake." I'm blinking my eyes and looking at the blades of grass growing between my fingers. Probably growing as we speak. I look back up at George.

"Dirt is everywhere. This tree grows in dirt. We're all dirt…made my lunch…."

"Not dirt. Dirk, Blake. Listen to me. Where is Dirk?"

"Oh shit. What did I say? Dirt? That's retarded. Shit, that is retarded."

Temple scampers over stacks of pages and books in the computer room. I slant back in the banana chair. Rock. To sit in the chair your legs must support you. It takes effort to sit still. Rock back, roll forth. Temple comes back again. Now Luna has jumped onto my chest. Her little face is too small for her head. This is ridiculous.

A little-faced cat makes no sense. Looks at me and put put puts under the table supporting my computer. My desk. The computer is empty. Like an unsharpened pencil. Similes don't help now. Temple under the table. And a man on a banana. The cold stare. My flesh tingles, energy moving away from the core, like my spirit is leaving me. But that doesn't cut it. In Hawaii Annie probably sits on a beach somewhere sipping mini-bar bottles. Or maybe she's fighting with her parents. When she thinks about me, she wants to....

Writing a description of something is not creation. I don't want to have to look forward, but all I do is stare. I stare at the floor. The carpet needs to be vacuumed. I need to make a long distance phone call.

I slip off the chair and pull myself back up. The alcohol will win this battle. But alcohol alone couldn't sink this boat. I bugged Dirk for that pill...I could go to bed and deal with it in the morning. I'm too tired to think straight. I can't...think. Muscles get heavy and the floor pulls you to it. This time I lie on the floor. The room is absolutely silent except for the noise outside. And Temple's purring. Or maybe little-faced Luna. Right by my ear. She lies against me. The the sloth...the the...often little moon how I look to you. Register my sins. What I wouldn't give to be able to cry right now. I believe if I could cry right now, my wounds would heal. My mistakes. I don't have a CD for this. All of it makes sense and suddenly I am convicted...my conviction that drives me, that excuses transgressions. Letting the floor slip away.... I don't want to sleep on the floor. Cramped between a banana chair and a basket full of Annie's papers. My feet might be kicking bills. Tomorrow. I'm going to clean this floor. After I sleep in....

# BLAKE (AUGUST 9, 2005)

The cashier's booth is a tiny room with a large window that looks into the kitchen at the in-room dining table line. It has a door that can be closed if the phones are busy to combat the kitchen noise, but typically is left propped open for ventilation. There is one stool, one chair, and one wastepaper basket packed in fifteen square feet. The room has a single counter for the two phones and two computers. Most evening shifts Sonja sits on the stool flipping through a small-press feminist magazine occasionally taking an order when the phones ring. When the shifts are slow the servers will slip into the booth to sit in the empty chair or use the telephones for personal calls.

I cover the phones while Sonja uses the restroom. With the hotel's low occupancy they have rung twice in the three hours I have been at work. I flip the pages of one of Sonja's magazines and skim an article that explicates the sexist tactics used by several large corporate magazine sponsors. The ads, one for a fast-food chain and one for an oil company, portray women in what the article calls, "traditional roles of patriarchic dominance and sexual subjectivity."

I call home while flipping the pages of the magazine. Annette answers the phone.

"Hey, Dolls," I say.

"Hello, Doll," she says. "When are you coming home?"

"Well, hello to you, too," I say.

"I'm serious," she says. "You haven't had a day off in over a week."

"I know, I know," I say. "It sucks, because the hotel is slow, but they still need to schedule me to cover while Dirk is out of town."

"I don't care," Annette says. "They should hire more people if you need to work that much."

"I know, right?" I close the magazine and look through the window at the kitchen. "At least I'm getting hours. Anyway, Pedro is supposed to come in at six, so I should be off pretty soon after that."

There is silence on the other side of the line, and I ask if Annette is still there.

"Yeah…that's fine. Just come home soon," she says.

"I will, Dolls. I'll bring burgers. Love you." I hang up the phone and five seconds later it rings with a guest order.

At 11:30 P.M., I step out of my car and walk across the apartment complex parking lot noting that some asshole threw his fast food wrappers on the ground. One of the large plastic globes that fit over the walkway lamps has been knocked off its post and the naked light bulb is somehow less illuminant. There is an empty Bud Light bottle on the lawn. My back and legs hurt, and I think I have to take a crap.

I open the front door slowly, careful not to let Temple or Luna run outside. They eye me from the incomplete couch, and I step inside. The light is on, but Annette is in the bedroom with the door closed. In the front room the floor has been vacuumed and the mess of shredded magazines (compliments of Temple) have been picked up. Our incomplete couch (the couch created out of couch cushions without a frame) has been stacked neatly and the little orange tool box that serves as our table is clean and topped with a three-in-one scented candle.

Temple skips off the couch and scurries across the front room. She nuzzles against my legs and slithers between my shoes. I give her a good rub and walk toward the bedroom. The light is off and Annette lies in bed watching TV. She doesn't look up.

I crawl onto our bed and push my face into her neck and talk to her in my baby voice.

*"Hey, Dolls."*

"Don't," she says and elbows me away.

*"Don't, Dolls. I just had the worst night."*

"I don't care," she says. "You could have called."

*"I couldn't call, Dolls."* I push my face back into her neck. "I have been running non-stop since I got off the phone with you. We got slammed. A basketball team came in and the only two guys running orders were me and Pedro."

"Where have you really been?" she asks.

"Oh, don't start this."

"What?" she says. "What have you really been doing? Who were you with?"

"This shit is so stupid," I say. "You honestly think I've been out with someone else? For Christ's sake, smell me. I smell like a kitchen garbage can. What are you watching?" I hate late night talk shows.

"I called your work, and they said you left," she says.

"Bullshit, when did you call? I was there until about a half hour ago. What time did you call?"

"..."

"I'm going to take a shower," I say. I undress in the hallway and shower with the door open. Temple sits on the toilet lid and watches me.

# BLAKE (AUGUST 19, 2005)

Charly lies upside down in the eight-foot bean bag deseeding the clumps of pot in a little baggie above his head that sits on the hard plastic floor-mat. I sit in a silver and purple banana chair next to him rocking back and forth trying to take my body weight off my legs. Nate slumps back into his inflatable Britney Spears chair. Across the room the television plays music videos.

Last year Charly, Nate, and Tyler deliberately threw out their real furniture in an act of "defiance against the bourgeois." In the center of the room a large plastic floormat, typically used in offices for rolling chairs, serves as their coffee table. Heavy metal posters adorn the walls (the Misfits skull, an old Sabbath poster, Iron Maiden, etc...).

I turn to Nate and ask where Tyler is.

"He's working," says Nate.

"It's like 7:30 P.M. on a Friday night. He's still at the mill, isn't he? Why is he at work?" I ask.

"They have a big order. He's been working like sixty hours a week the last couple of weeks," Nate says.

"Boo-ya," says Charly. He rolls his legs over in a backward somersault onto the mat. "This should be ready to go." He jogs over to the kitchen to grab the bong. With the bong in his right hand, he imitates an Irish jig dancing back to us while singing, "Quentin's on his waaay with another jaaay and it's okaaaay...."

"Suh-weet," says Nate sitting forward in his chair.

Charly kneels down next to the baggy and begins to pack a bowl. "What are we doing tonight?" he asks me. I shrug. Earlier Annette told me she was going out with her sister and her sister's friends. I was on my own.

Charly turns to Nate and says, "It's Friday. We've got to do something." Nate doesn't say anything, so Charly turns back to the bowl deflated. He half-heartedly jabs the bits of pot into the bowl. "How lame...we should at least pick up some beer."

"I can make some phone calls," Nate says.

"Yeah?" asks Charly. "Well, that's a start. Make some calls. It's Friday."

Nate takes his cell phone out of his pocket. Charly puts his mouth to the end of the bong, holds his lit Zippo to the bowl, and inhales. He holds his breath and then coughs while nodding and says, "It's good. Who's next?"

"I'm out. They're supposed to have randoms at my work this week," I say.

"What?" says Charly. "You think taking a week off is going to make a difference?"

I mumble that I don't know and then check the time on my phone again. Nate takes the bong from Charly. Through the haze of weed smoke, I read the digital VCR clock and decide I want to make the beer run. I'm about to stand up when a Phoenix video comes on the television.

"Holy shit that's Phoenix," I say pointing to the

television screen.

Nate turns to the TV and then says, "Yep. His video has been on a bunch."

I mumble to myself that I didn't even know he made music videos, while my eyes are transfixed by the screen. Phoenix is one of a group of do-it-yourself underground emcees to become popular through internet networking. These artists all shun what they refer to as "typical mainstream marketability" and pride themselves on presenting "alternative intellectual" content in their lyrics. On the photos from his homemade album cases, Phoenix fashions himself as a Templar knight and describes his mission as one of "intellectual historical revisionism."

"This is brilliant," I say again pointing, taking my eyes off the screen only for a second to look at Charly and Nate.

Charly turns to the screen for a second and then back to the bong. "Yep," he says.

"I'm falling apart here," I say. I know that next time I see that video I probably won't be as captivated, but I don't want that to happen yet. For this moment I want to believe that my enthusiasm will last. That my sensitivity won't be lost, and I won't need something new to interest me. That something I cherish can last. Won't be forgotten in twenty minutes.

So then I go make that beer run.

# BLAKE (OCTOBER 22, 2005)

Charly is supposed to have my orange juice. On the plastic floormat in front of me sits two-thirds of a bottle of Vox vodka. I'm alone in the front room of the condo, prostrate across the eight foot bean bag chair watching a TV show where overpaid comics comment on celebrity incidences from the day. The show is called "Ten Minutes Ago..." and is marketed as "Immediate celebrity reportage." The format of the show includes a voiceover narrator that will say, "Ten minutes ago Blank Blank stumbled on her stiletto," while the screen shows the paparazzi footage of this event. The scene will then cut to talking heads of comedians who provide color commentary. Ten minutes ago Jerry Seinfeld received a parking ticket on his $150,000 Porsche in front of a Jane's Java while he was inside the café breaking a ten-dollar bill to put change in the parking meter. The footage shows the meter maid shake her head at Jerry who pleads, "Come on."

*As if Jerry Seinfeld can't afford to pay a twenty-dollar parking ticket. Here's an actor who made one million dollars an episode twenty-two times a year bickering over a twenty-dollar ticket....*

Nate walks in the room with a glass in his hand. He looks at the bottle of vodka and then at me and says, "How are you dealing with life?"

"Is Charly back yet?" I ask.

"I thought you were waiting for orange juice," Nate says. He picks up the bottle of vodka and shakes it.

I shrug and say, "The doctor is *In.*" Ten minutes ago millionaire heiress Paris Hilton was asked her name by the bouncer of an A-list soiree in New Orleans.

*You're employed to screen celebrities at the reportedly hottest club in one of this country's party capitals and you don't recognize the queen of fame?*

"Get that?" says Nate. "Employed to screen celebrities and you don't even know Paris Hilton! Ha ha, get that!"

"Why are we watching this?"

Neither of us changes the channel. After two more celebrity tragedies Charly returns with the orange juice.

"Damn, someone wasn't in a hurry," I say.

"Taco craving, bro. Life goes on," Charly says and sets the orange juice next to the Vox. He and Nate divide their Mexican food across the plastic floormat while I pour myself a heavy screwdriver.

"You pass me that?" asks Charly. I hand him the bottle of Vox. He tilts it up and swallows two large gulps before putting it down again. Looking at my face he asks, "What? You don't drink for the flavor?"

I smile. How does Charly tick? He's definitely the most concentrated of whatever this condo houses. I once watched Charly jump off the roof of a garage into the bed of a slowly driving truck. He did this while completely intoxicated for four dollars. At a club's opening night he threw up on the dance floor, because he wanted to disgust the girls wearing sandals. And then there was the party in the Park City townhome where he deliberately pissed his pants, so he could leave a stain on the girl's couch who owned the place. He wasn't even drunk, sitting there with a pillow over his lap and the most maniacal smile. His anger was twisted to a perverse politics.

"Why the fuck are we watching this?" Charly asks.

Nate says Charly changed after the two years he lived in California holding the spit bucket for his mom, while she died of breast cancer. Before that, Charly hadn't seen his mom since she left his father when Charly was fifteen. This was something you didn't talk about. You never heard anything about Charly's mom, and then one day he had moved to California. I didn't know anyone was even in touch with him, but occasionally Nate read us updated tales from handwritten letters. When Charly came back to live with Nate and Tyler, no one asked him about it.

Charly turns off the TV, and we drink for another hour. I feel the vodka peel me, the warmth spreads and loosens. We sit around the plastic floormat playing quarters with Black Sabbath blaring out of the stereo. I haven't touched the orange juice for some time. Tyler is home from work and cuts through a thirty-pack of beer with Charly and Nate's aid.

When Tyler's phone rings he stands up from the plastic to answer it.

"Sit back down, bitch," says Nate.

"Chelsea? What's going on?" Tyler says with one hand over his ear. "No, let me go into the kitchen," he says into the phone.

"He's assing out," I say. I bounce a quarter, but it hits the edge of the glass in front of me and doesn't go in.

"Let me help you," says Charly. He tries to bounce the quarter into the glass in front of me, but it doesn't go in either. "We'll keep a running tab."

In the kitchen we hear Tyler flirting with Chelsea. Tyler talks to more girls than the rest of us combined. I've never been able to figure that out. He comes back in from the kitchen pointing at us with both hands.

We are packed into Charly's Bronco. I realize in this blaring club music, Charly knocking the beat into the steering wheel, and the rushing air over the topless Bronco isolating us from the outside world, that I am drunk enough to romanticize everything. Maybe it's the camaraderie of piling together into close quarters on a single mission. Maybe it's the joy of having an infinite number of possibilities for the night.

"Who is Chelsea?" I ask Nate.

"We've hung out with these girls before." The wind plus the music makes it hard to hear him. "They share a house above Wasatch, like four of them. Tyler met her at a restaurant. Some strange may do you some good."

When we reach the bench, the valley below looks like a glittering bedspread. In the south the valley's lights spread in street patterns: an illuminated patchwork, but the more downtown one looks, the density clusters like we're trailing a comet north of us. I know I won't be alone forever, but it would be easier if I had a way to learn her name....

Primarily everyone is split between a small but well-decorated living room and the back porch. The alcohol-less kitchen is a necropolis of empty liquor bottles and used Dixie cups. The blender pitcher sits on top of various dishes in the sink. A few lime wedges remain on the cutting board. There is no more liquor in the fridge or in any of the cabinets.

Charly smokes outside with a few guys we know from high school. Tyler has vanished into one of the bedrooms to smoke. Nate and I sit on a leather couch in the living room. Two girls sit in chairs opposite us with two of their friends on the floor between them. A guy I know from high school named Nick sits on the floor and intermittently beats on a bongo drum in his lap to the music playing on the stereo.

"I've been doing tile work," says Nick. "Any monkey can do it, but the pay's decent, and I'm clocking over fifty hours a week."

"That's good," says Nate. "Right now construction is really slow out here. My dad has guys calling him all the time to come work for him. They have their own construction companies, and they'll work for him for ten dollars an hour. My dad's like the only one who has any business."

"He must be doing well."

"All right. He's saving to get a new Tacoma truck."

"You should see B.J.'s truck. It's the Beast. When I drive behind him I can see the cars in front of him *from underneath it....*"

I can't make out the conversation either of the girls are having, but it appears that the girl on the floor next to the girl in one of the chairs, the short brunette, is having boyfriend trouble. I hear the olive-skinned brunette sitting on the chair say, "but you had to expect that after how he was with Jen." Both of the girls are pretty committed to not looking over toward my couch. On the other chair a chin-length, platinum blonde talks to a girl with long dirty-blond hair. I have no clue as to what they are saying.

"...tried riding up Lion's Back once and about thirty yards up the Jeep locks. We had to back down and I was shitting my pants..." says Nate.

The platinum blonde is the skinniest, but her features are a little sharp. She will make a fantastic MILF. For some reason it is easy to imagine her with a little blond child on her hip while cheering on another one on a Saturday soccer afternoon. Her dirty blond friend has bad skin and bad features. Her t-shirt and ruffle skirt aren't working or hurting. I bet she smokes. The brunette in the chair has nice tits and a low-cut shirt. Her olive skin and expensive clothing make me think she is not going to be interested in my bohemian lifestyle. She is the type of girl who likes bourgeois luxuries like microwaves, toasters, and TV's. The girl with boyfriend trouble is the best all-around catch, but obviously has enough baggage with her relationship.

"You've been to Nate's condo," Nick says this to the girl with the olive skin.

"I...."

"I know you've been there, Jessica. The place off thirteenth. He lives with Tyler Main."

"Yeah, OK. Maybe last fall. How's it going?" she asks Nate.

"Quite well." Nate is smiling. "You live here?"

"With Shelly," she nods to the platinum blonde, "and Chelsea. We've been renting it for like two months."

"How did you guys find it?" asks Nate.

"Shelly cuts the hair of the woman who owns it."

"You work at a salon?" I say.

Nate keeps talking to Jessica.

"It's probably time to cut your hair," Nick says to me. Nick has short spiky hair.

Shelly laughs.

"I haven't had my hair cut by a professional for over a decade," I say. "I just shave it when it gets long."

There is an awkward silence. Nick attempts to beat a couple of lavish drum rolls, and I stand and go talk to Charly.

This tired night a swimming sea all rolling with the guitar chords I'm striking in my head. The tip tip tip tip bash beating and this song rips into a solo. My piss drip drip drip drip down the tree trunk and into the foliage. Walking back around the porch everyone's together huddled. I throw my arms around Nate calling Here's the man with teeth like God's shoe shine. Nate is pointing to other parts of Charly's shoes so he can be sure and spray those better. Nick and some of the other guys are laughing. Tyler talks around the joint in his mouth and says to one of the girls Dis's uh shit, bitch! He sparkles, shimmers, and shines. Nate explains that Charly is spraying his shoes with hair spray.

"Is that some of your hair spray?" I ask Shelly. She either ignores me or has been talking to her friend the whole time. I tell myself I wouldn't like a flat chick anyway. It's the hip hop in my veins. I need some ruuummmp, cuuunnt. Charly is tying his shoes. And then stands up straight.

"Anyone got a lighter?"

"Allow me," says Tyler. He leans over and ashes his joint over Charly's shoes. Good Night! There is a camera flash, and Charly is off running circles around the backyard. I jump up and down. Yeah! Yeah! Yeah! Nate is hooting. The dirty blonde has her hands over her open mouth.

Charly is wooh wooh woohing around the grass and then attempts to stamp his foot out with his other foot, but to no avail. When he realizes they're not going out he yells fuck and runs around the side of the house.

We yell shit into the shit sky and chase him, down the street these bouncing fireballs leading away. And then they vanish. The sprinklers save Charly. Nate and I attempt to put him on our shoulders, but fail and run back to the party with an awkwardly carried Charly. It's the sprinklers, the sprinklers. Look at his shoes. The molten rubber and plastic breaking off in chips. Shelly says, You're bleeding. You're bleeding.

I wake up lying on the carpet next to my computer chair. My head is in between my banana chair and a pair of Annette's jeans I found stuffed in the cushions of the incomplete couch. It's the only article of Annette's clothing that I have left.

I should stand and see what time it is. It's light outside. Another second passes and the throbbing in my head reaches a new level. Simultaneously I recognize the pain and realize it's been there for hours. The awareness makes it worse. I peer up to my computer table and see Luna walking over what has to be my keyboard. She shouldn't be up there. Temple moves near my feet and nips at my toes causing me to twitch.

"Damn cats."

Luna meows. She jumps down from the table and begins walking over me back and forth threatening to sit her asshole right onto my nose.

"Luna. *Luna.*"

I aggressively pet her keeping that asshole away from my nose. She paces my torso. I reach over and pick up the telephone.

"Thank you for calling the Grand National—"

"Hey, Janelle, it's Blake. I'm totally sick and can't come into today. Sorry."

"Are you OK?"

"Yeah, totally sick. Tell them I'm on the brink of death, OK? Thanks."

It can't be that late in the day. Janelle works morning shifts, plus the cats would have eaten if I didn't get up sooner. I should have asked what time it is. I reach for the remote control to my stereo. It doesn't turn on when I push Power. I sit myself up halfway and attempt to click the button at a better angle. Damn it. I hunch over and nausea courses through me. The button still won't give. I open the back of the remote control and find that Annette removed the batteries.

# BLAKE (MAY 7, 2005)

I drive Annette to the gully for a picnic. I park in the lower parking lot, near the playground, so that we can sit on the manicured lawn in the shade of one of the few trees. We unfold a blanket and spread our bounty, goods from a specialty produce and dairy market. In the shade, the sun is still warm, but a cool breeze blows from the canyon, and with it, a lingering trace of winter's ice. We are alone on the field, but in the distance a colony of children run in the sand scrambling into and out of the playground. Their cries, screams, and cheers drown out the sound of the highway on the other side of the park.

Sitting cross-legged, Annette reaches for a foil-wrapped cylinder of brie. "Do you want some brie? It's a 'Double-Cream Specialty?'" she reads from the label with particular relish, while she picks at the foil with her fingernails. Annette has her newly dyed black hair pulled into a ponytail and, with her Summer tan, appears so dark to me that I fantasize I have stolen Tiger Lily away from Captain Hook. She wears light pink short shorts and a loose white t-shirt. My black t-shirt reads, "The Last Star

Writer" in white letters, and I wear khaki shorts and skate shoes with no socks. I can feel the blades of grass tickle my ankles when my feet hang off the blanket. To my right is a Frisbee and soccer ball. There is also a paddle ball game called Crush Ball that I bought at a grocery store for two dollars.

"No. Maybe a pear," I say.

"An organically-grown, Bartlett pear?" she asks. She smiles and hands me the pear. She takes out a loaf of French bread and spreads some brie over a slice. I open the bottle of wine, but leave it in the paper bag. The wine is a good cabernet, and I sip it trying to taste something more than just the wine. I want to taste things in the wine.

"Do you want some of this?" I pass her the bottle, and she takes a steady gulp. I wonder if she can taste things.

"What is it?" she asks.

*"C'est un cabernet sauvignon.* You like it?" I take a bite of the pear, and the texture seems tough. I look at the pear, but I can't tell if it is ripe. It tastes sweet, but I don't think of quicksand. The texture of pears always reminds me of quicksand.

"..."

"I'm so glad I didn't have to work today. I think it's the first Saturday I've had off in maybe two months." My room service schedule has been erratic. Annette nannies three kids Monday through Friday eight-to-six.

"It seems like we never hang out anymore. I see you when I wake up for work and you're sleeping, or you come home when I'm sleeping," she says.

"It doesn't have to be like that," I say. "You don't have to work as much as you do. It's not like you're saving the money anyway, you should just tell them you can only work certain days."

"It doesn't work like that. Maybe if you had a better job, and we could actually afford things, I wouldn't have to work so much."

"My job is fine. We make way more money than we need. If you saved as much as I save—"

"Yes, it's all my fault, we're broke." Annette begins cutting another slice of bread. I take the bottle of wine and have a sip.

"What does that mean?"

"Let me tell you a secret. My parents are rich, and the best way to get rich is to make more money. Not live like a homeless person until you die."

"We hardly live like homeless people," I say.

I cut myself a slice of bread and have some cheese. The wine is about half gone. It's only two in the afternoon and the sun is still warm. I lie on the blanket and a bug buzzes around my face, so I sit back up.

"Do you want to play some Crush Ball?" I ask.

"OK," she says.

We play this game for fifteen minutes spending most of the time picking the ball up from the lawn, and then we sit back down for some more wine.

"This is a fun game for two dollars," I say.

She shrugs.

"It's better than a movie," I say.

"Scott and Amy saw *One Armed Scissor*," she says. "They said it was good."

"How do they get money to go to movies? Every time they call and invite us over, I'm amazed they've paid rent another month."

"Their parents help them out. They do chores and stuff for Scott's parents and watch the kids. And I think they take care of Amy's parents' yard."

"What are they going to do when the grass stops

growing?" I ask.

"Shovel snow or something, probably," she says. "They find ways."

"Doesn't make sense to me." I feel warm so I set the bottle of wine down. "Do you want some of this?" She shakes her head. I lie back on the blanket and stretch my arms above me. Leaves move in the sunlight kaleidoscoping the shade. On the playground it looks like some of the kids are playing tag. "Wine makes me lazy."

Annette lies against me with her head on my chest.

"Do you think we'll always be poor?" she asks.

I rub the side of her arm. "We're not poor." A teacher or babysitter gathers up the children at the playground to take them away.

"Can't you write a book or something?"

"Maybe if you were a better muse."

"I can't turn dog pee into gold."

It's a stupid, weird line, but the fact that she is the type of girl who would use the word "pee" arouses me. I wonder if once the children leave the playground, anyone could see us from the park road or the highway. Unlikely from the highway.

"I'm hungry," I say. I begin rubbing her back harder and feel her pulled against me. I can feel the warmth of her back on my arm.

"Have a Braeburn apple," she says.

"I want man food," I say.

"Do you want to go somewhere to get food?" She turns her face toward me. I delicately pull the back of her shirt up one finger stride at a time.

"No. I'm just hungry."

My middle finger reaches the edge of her shirt and then her skin.

"What? Do you want to get something or not?"

"For the cost of food, I'd rather enjoy my hunger," I say.

"I can't believe I live with you."

Rubbing her back with my fingertips, I slip my fingers under the elastic of her shorts' waistband.

"What are you doing?" she asks.

"What are you thinking?"

She props herself onto her elbow.

"We can't do anything here," she says.

"What about over there?"

"On the swings?"

"In the tube slide."

"A blow job?" she asks.

"No," I say and rub her back. "Let's have sex."

"It won't work," she says.

"Don't be a sissy." We sit up. Her bangs fall over to the side like a wave's curl. I love that. "Come on. Let's do it," I say.

She shrugs, and we walk over to the empty playground.

Before we step into the sand, I look around and say, "Do you think anyone can see us?"

"Oh now who's a sissy?"

"I'm just saying."

We walk over and look at the tube slide. The entire slide is maybe eight to ten feet long. The diameter of the tube is wide enough to pass a child sitting upright.

"How do you want to do this?" Annette asks. I look at her and shrug and then crouch down by the opening of the tube and look up it.

"It kind of smells. I hope no one peed in it."

"Probably at least once," she says.

"Gross." I climb in, and stretch myself up the slide. I roll onto my back, but the hard rubber is slippery and in order to stay on the incline I have to prop my right foot against the top of the slide.

"OK. How do I get in?"

"Come around the top of the slide," I say. I can hear her walk around the playground and up the wooden platforms. Looking out the top of the slide, I can see blinding blue and then her upside down face.

"How am I going to fit in that?"

"Just climb on top of me."

"You've got to be kidding me. Your leg is in the way."

"It won't be in the way. Just crawl down on top of me feet first." I can hear her mumble that this is ridiculous as she crouches and begins to stick her leg into the slide.

"Wait," I say. I undo my shorts and slide them down as much as I can. "Just getting ready. Go ahead." As she begins to slide over me I realize how tight our fit is. Her weight grinds me. We have trouble keeping ourselves from slipping down the slide.

She stares right into my face and asks, "Is this going to work?"

"I don't know."

I feel her hand reaching for my penis.

"You're not even ready," she says.

"I'm sorry this isn't the most stimulating environment I've ever been in."

"Well, get ready."

"I can't. I'm holding us up so we don't slide down," I say.

"Do you want me to?" she asks. I feel awkward yanks and tugs.

"Agh, that's not going to work. Tell me something sexy."

"What do you want to hear?" she asks. In the tube slide, the acoustics of our voices are magnified.

Everything sounds like loud whispers.

"Tell me about the first guy you went down on," I say.

"We were at school, and we went out to his car—"

"How old were you?" I ask.

"Fourteen," she says, "and he was eighteen...." She begins telling the story, and I can feel my nerves start to tingle. In my imagination Annette looks exactly the same, only she's younger. And has to be wearing a school uniform skirt. The nameless boy has no face. No real body. Only direction and it is back at her. I can feel her on top of me.

"OK," I say, "let's do it."

We make an attempt.

"It's not going to work. I'm not ready."

"Fuck."

"Wait a second." She licks her fingers and her hand disappears.

"HURRY UP, DAD," calls a girl's voice from around the playground.

"Oh shit," I whisper. We can hear little footsteps run around the playground in the sand.

"What should we do?" Annette asks.

"Run. Get out." I push Annette out the top of the slide awkwardly and go sliding down. My shorts are still around my knees and my erection stands tall. Because of my height in the children's slide, I can't sit up at the bottom and have to push myself feet-first out of the tube. I land butt-flat in the sand staring eye-to-eye with a six year-old blond girl. Behind her stands her father, maybe ten years older than I am, smoking a cigarette, wearing jeans and a red flannel shirt. They both stare at me dumbfounded. I jump to my feet and pull my pants up. At the top of the slide Annette waves to the two of them and says, "Hello."

I run from the playground back to our lunch things and grab everything. Annette catches up to me at the car, and we drive away.

# BLAKE (OCTOBER 23, 2005)

Sick, I stumble out of bed. Luna follows me into the bathroom because my bathroom is too small for me to stand in front of the toilet and simultaneously shut the door. I begin pissing, and Luna hops onto the back of the toilet.

"No shame in your game," I say aloud. Luna doesn't look at my face while I say this.

She concentrates on my pissing and I worry she is going to swipe at either my stream or me. She leans forward with her paw on the upright toilet seat. I watch the toilet seat slowly begin to slip forward and little Luna's paw slip off the seat as she begins a slow descent. I'm watching this half-sober about one second faster than I can react to it. The toilet seat knocks through my stream in one tight splashburst chiming the opening note to a symphony of seat banging, kitten in bowl urine-splashing, and a horrified, hung-over gasp.

I run through my apartment with a urine-soaked kitten in my right hand while my left hand works my boxers back to my waist. I just want to make it to the door. I swing open the front door to my apartment, and, while attempting to throw the urine-soaked kitten from my apartment, I trip over the doorjamb and fall onto my porch. My nausea from drinking and the urine smell getting the best of me, I vomit right in front of my door stoop, half-naked, as my neighbors walk past, dressed to go to church.

# BLAKE (JUNE 10, 2005)

With the sun beading on us with its full ninety degrees, the vigor of early Summer, my brow wrinkled and pushing sweat, the two pre-adolescents swinging their stubby legs out of the double-stroller that weighs like a boulder on the steep side of this poured-concrete path, I decide, yes, this is worse than room service, worse than simultaneously pushing three tables down a long hallway of plush carpet, the combined weight of the tables about five hundred pounds distributed over twelve five-inch plastic wheels. This is worse than the combined smell of stale grease and dirty dishwater. I am at the zoo trying to decide how it was my turn to push the kids in the double-stroller, trying to decide why the zoo must have so many short and steep hills to push strollers up, and trying to decide what is the reason that not one single tree could spread a branch over this brutal stretch of path and maybe briefly interrupt the sun's struggle to give me cancer. I decide I can't push this stroller any farther while walking.

"Do you want to wait up?" says Annette from behind.

She carries the nine-month old Hailey Jade on her left hip.

Without wasting a breath in response, I push the stroller hard enough to make the bearings on the stroller's wheels sing. The two-year old, Jason, holds his tiny hands into the breeze from our acceleration and says, "Wooo." I keep my elbows locked straight, push my head down and stare at my running feet and the concrete passing beneath them, bringing us ever closer to the crest of this miserable hill. And then the hill levels, and my energy drops, and I park us next to a patch of grass with a short wooden fence around it in front of the House of Butterflies. A large peacock sits in the grass. Jason tries to look below the wooden pole I sit on, while Jenny, the four-year old, explains that male peacocks have the pretty feathers to attract females. Annette makes her way up the hill, and I can sense her glare through her sunglasses.

"Maybe you don't need to run off," she says.

My first impulse is to tell her to go to hell: I'm here hanging out with her on my day off, while she nannies kids, and besides why did I have to push the stroller up that? Instead I say, "It's so hot today. I need to get out of the sun."

"You could take Jenny through the House of Butterflies. I'll stay out here with Jason and Hailey."

"You want to see the butterflies?" I ask Jenny.

"Yeah!"

"E'phant counter," says Jason.

"We already saw the Elephant Encounter," says Annette.

I unbuckle Jenny from the stroller and take her by the hand through the double doors of the butterfly house. Inside we follow a narrow path that winds back and forth through the damp aviary. On one side a manmade waterfall spills seven feet into a creek that winds throughout the aviary and underneath the path. I expected more butterflies. Also more variety; for every one black or blue butterfly, I see fifty of the same orange.

"Jenny, do you like the butterflies?"

"Where's the caterpillars?"

"I don't think they have caterpillars," I say. I move left and right across the path reading the little information signs, but none of them give me the name of the orange butterfly. Behind me a family pushes a stroller up on my heels, and I keep taking Jenny by the hand to make sure she walks forward, though we can't move ahead of the slow-moving family in front of us. The family behind us pushes to our heels and then we push to the family in front of us, who push to the next family. For some reason, everyone is overweight.

"ALL BUTTERFLIES WERE CATERPILLARS."

"What?" I ask.

"All butterflies were caterpillars."

"Don't touch any of...I think they still count as butterflies even if they are in the caterpillar stage," but Jenny shakes her head near a flower so that her hair disturbs a butterfly and it flies off. She doesn't listen to me. I look around and wish I knew the name of all these orange butterflies....

Outside, my damp shirt sticks to my skin.

Fidgeting with my shirt I ask Annette, "Is there steam coming off me? That place is like standing in a shower."

"You sure were in there a long time." Annette has Hailey Jade on her lap, and Jason and Jenny are standing by the fence looking at the peacock.

"You can't get ahead of anyone in there. We got stuck behind a family of fat people...and so many strollers." Annette sets Hailey Jade into the stroller and buckles her in.

"Where do you want to go next?" I ask.

"We should get them food," she says. "Come here Jason."

"No 'Nette. I ca' walk."

"Come here." Annette grabs him by the arm and Jason screams.

"Maybe he could walk for a bit," I say.

"I don't want him running off," says Annette over Jason's tantrum as she buckles him into the stroller.

At a concession stand with a Tiki motif and koala hats I pay twenty dollars for four hotdogs, two bags of chips, and two cokes (the two *meals* save me money). Annette hands each of the kids a hotdog and starts feeding Hailey a bottle. I finish my hotdog, and Annette gives her chips to Jason. Both Jason and Jenny start working on the chips and neither finishes their hotdog. Annette takes my chips, but when I protest she hands me her hotdog. I throw away most of two hotdogs and half a bag of chips, more than a quarter of our lunch.

After eating, we sit at the picnic tables and rest. I look up at the tree branches above my head that blow around enough to barely intercept the sunlight. The combination of soda, sunlight, and sweat make my stomach sore, and on a light breeze that passes, I catch the faint trace of wild feces. Annette bounces Hailey Jade on her lap lightly to make her smile, and I become concerned that Hailey will vomit. When I ask Annette if that is wise to do right after feeding the baby, she casts me a look that says if-you-question-my-work-again-I-will-slap-you-in-public. I look at Jason and Jenny. Jason's face is red, and he rubs his little hand over his eyes. He says, "Firsty, 'Nette," which translates into Annette giving him her soda. In a few minutes, because it's hot, Annette takes mine.

While pushing the stroller again up and down pointless rises and dips in the path, I wonder if Annette is going to reimburse me for the money I spent on lunch. Annette is being paid to do this and the lunch cost twelve dollars more than my admission ticket. I push the stupid stroller everywhere; and, for all of the forestry that surrounds the paths at the zoo, I still can't find a decent patch of shade.

Through the large window on one side of the Large Primate complex I see a stout gorilla walk down the grassy incline. I don't know how to distinguish between male and female gorillas, but this one has a bubble butt and the chest and arms of a wrestler. The gorilla walks up to the window and for one moment it is closer to us than any animal has been our entire visit. During this brief second, neither Jason nor Jenny responds with much enthusiasm, and the gorilla, as if trained, entirely ignores our presence. It walks past the window and stops just out of our line of sight.

"That gorilla is shorter than I expected," I say.

"According to the sign it can snap three-inch bamboo stalks with little effort."

"That should be a show."

We walk around its enclosure, and I see two ten-year old boys leaning their heads over the four-and-a-half-foot wall. Peering over the side I see a gorilla fifteen feet below them lying on its back with its head against the wall staring up into the sky. It appears to look beyond our eyes, and I hear the refrain of one of the boys, "Yeah, but don't. Don't spit on him. Don't."

# BLAKE (NOVEMBER 5, 2005)

Nate and I sit in the Urban Lounge in a booth behind the speakers and maintain a screaming conversation.

"I can't even *read* anymore, there's no way I'm going to be able to sit still enough to write anything," I say.

"I think all of this could be really good for you," says Nate. "I mean, don't write about this stuff...but if you write about something else, I think all of this passion or heart or whatever will come out."

I shrug and take a drink from my stein. On stage a garage rock band I recognize, but can never remember the name of, plays a song with almost no melody. And then once they play through the whole song, they repeat it again.

"I'm serious," says Nate. "The last scene I wrote in my novel begins," Nate lifts his right hand up and waves his pointer finger as if conducting a symphony while quoting, "'The first week after my laser eye surgery, my doctor told me that I could expect my vision to steadily improve as my eyes healed. By the end of the first month, I could see into people's souls.'" He puts his hand down and then says, "And then I go on to describe how this guy has to deal with the double burden of being a human and having a godlike ability." Nate sits back in the booth and takes a drink from his Cape Cod.

"How is what you're writing even a novel?" I ask.

"It's a novel, because on the front of the book I will call it a novel. I promise, even though all of this crazy stuff is going on, these characters interact in the same world."

"You've had the guy who wants to be a knight interact with the laser guy eye...laser eye guy?"

"Well, no, but—"

"Have you had two single scenes share characters from a different scene?"

"They refer to each other," says Nate with some attitude. "For instance, look at this scene with the laser eye guy: basically he's the equivalent of a super hero. It's not that hard to make a transition to a character that wishes he were a super hero."

"I don't understand how looking into people's souls is the same thing as a super power."

"That's what is so great about all of that writing. When I actually describe what is going on it's not like the character knows at first what is happening either. He just knows that when he leans a certain way people's heads glow. Like certain colors start to stand out. This is where you bring in the whole mythos of people's auras and when people's health change their colors change. But I describe the whole thing like it's shadows. Out of his peripheral he senses it. It takes him a while to figure it out, because actually seeing the soul is not as literal as it sounds. First, you see or sense those colored shadows...or auras or halos—there's so many possibilities and subtexts. Then you start to half-experience and half-sense things. I got the idea from the movie *Unbreakable* when Bruce Willis brushes against people, and he can see what crimes they've committed. This is like that, except it's not that straightforward. You're not simply watching what someone did, but you're watching everything they wished they had done, the things they don't remember, things they remember differently, don't understand...wanted to and wished to do.... You see all that is their consciousness...and it is all instant...and constant. Of course my guy doesn't understand this right away. That would be, like, too much. Basic life in general is like that, anyway. What he does is learn how to absorb all of that and navigate his way through it. The trick is that it is all in a very physical sense and not a mental thing. Any time he tries to understand or think about what is going on he gets lost in the sensations. He has to actively learn...to be absolutely present or something...."

I stare at Nate and drink some beer for a minute. The band, whose name I can't remember, has finished its set, and a new band is setting up its gear.

"That sounds pretty good, but, like, it's its own thing and not a part of a novel," I say. "And what in the hell does that have to do with the fact that because of all of this Annette drama, I can't read or write anymore?"

"It will come out in your writing," says Nate. He sounds almost frustrated with me.

"Well, what in the hell is coming out in yours?"

"I want to be God," he says. He holds up his glass in a one-sided toast and takes a drink.

# TAYLOR (OCTOBER 22, 2005)

The heavy brick arches and sweaty stone walls in the basement of Divinity remind me of the all-ages punk shows and mosh pits I went to in high school. When we first come down the stairs we check the foldout merchandise table. Two men in their early twenties with dirty clothing and large backpacks covered in patches sit behind the table. They appear homeless, and one has glasses. The primary display is of the new Prestor John CD and stickers, but several Crimethink books and buttons dot the table as well. Andrew starts talking to one of the guys behind the table about the merits of dumpster diving behind chain pizza parlors. Dylan and I walk under one of the brick arches to the main chamber. Some guys and girls sit on top of the defunct bar near Dylan and me. On the far end of the large space three guys fiddle with the various piles of band equipment on the stage.

"I haven't been to a show in this place in forever," says Dylan.

"I swear, in high school, every band played in this stupid basement."

"We used to rally around that beam," says Dylan pointing. "I remember moshing to the ska bands."

"I wonder where Ian and them are?" I ask.

"They were under the stairs when we first came in."

"Really? I didn't know that," I say. I follow Dylan over to the corner of the basement under the stairs. Ian and the rest of Prestor John sit among some of their friends on the only three sofas in the basement. Their band equipment sits cased and piled in front of them like a musical campfire. A string of beige yarn sags between two rod-iron stanchions. In the center of the yarn is taped a piece of binder paper with thick crayon lettering that says, "Green Room."

"You're shitting me?" asks Dylan.

Ian smiles when we approach. "You guys made it," he says.

"What up? Is it alright if we cross the yarn?" I ask.

"Sit down," he says and slides over forcing a blank-faced girl to slide over as well. Ian is the taller of the two guitarists in Prestor John. He stylishly wears tight designer jeans and a skate t-shirt. His hair is dyed black and shaved into a faux hawk. The front of his hair has been bleached. I met Ian in an art class last year when I was the only other person in the class who had heard of Fugazi. We were the only two students to incorporate knife slashing as a canvas treatment.

"You pumped about the CD release?" I ask.

"I think it turned out really well. Have you guys heard it, yet?"

"No. You were going to show us the masters."

"Oh, yeah. Fuck," he says. "Just a second." Ian walks over to the merchandise table and comes back with a couple of CDs handing them to Dylan and me.

We thank him.

"We pulled Dave's guitar up and brought the mics up a little bit. It's not as experimental sounding, but the songs sound fuller."

"How'd you guys get this place?" I ask looking around.

"We used to come to punk shows here all the time when we were high school," says Dylan.

"It's a classic venue," Ian says.

"I'm pretty sure I have sketches of it in my old high school sketchbooks," I say.

"I was going to do a huge six foot by ten foot backdrop for our set, but I didn't get around to it," says Ian.

"One of those chunky, atmospheric pieces coffee shops like to hang on their walls and overprice?" I ask and smile.

"Actually I wanted to do a really classic, Baroque portrait of the band. Like a Rembrandt or something, but totally set in the period. I've still got the canvas."

"You should all be pirates in the painting," says Dylan.

"That's not really..." but Ian doesn't finish the sentence.

One of the guys in the opening band walks by and Ian calls to him, "Scott, how long until you guys are starting?"

"Jeremy's almost got his kit together; then we'll sound check." Scott walks away.

"Let me guess: gutter punk?" I say.

Ian shakes his head. "Brutal prog. Their bassist is one of Anthony's friends."

While staring at the crowd I see: the yellow basement light, spotlighting shoulders here, cheekbones there; a random youth aged fifteen to thirty caught mid-stride, laugh, and word; and ripped fabric in a variety of cotton-faded colors. I also see three various woolen sportcoats, brown khaki pants, khaki shorts, short skirts, and bright steel in bulbs, barbs, spikes, and rivets. The haunted, heavy profile stepping away from me toward this obscurity. The same dirty-blond, shoulder-length, flop. The stout, but still feminine-proportioned frame sporting a silken blouse, with a bright oriental pattern, and the misfit brown pants. It's in the combination of posture and lilt that I think I see Tara.

"I haven't moshed in a pit, since I was in high school," says Dylan.

"Just wait, people will full-on run circles around the pole," Ian says swirling his finger around.

"Then I want to crowd surf, hang-ten style. Like a Pearl Jam video."

"I've seen little girls crowd surf here. You'd be the first...dude," says Ian.

"If you guys pull the numbers, shouldn't be a problem. With enough people."

"I'd be worried about hitting my head."

"Fell on it once at a Bad Religion concert at Soltaire. Went right through a hole in the crowd," Dylan says.

"I mean, the ceiling. It's probably only about eight or nine feet high..." Ian says looking at the area in front of the stage on the other side of the brick arch.

There was a late afternoon sun with the light shadowing everything and hues shifting to a more intense yellow, unless you were sitting at one of the back tables of Muchachos with two friends facing across the valley through the large panel windows, then the light directly in your eyes was white. You were chewing on a Combination Burrito, oblivious to most other patrons, most everyone walking in the front doors when for only a brief second a couple, whose entrance you don't recall, draws enough attention by immediately exiting that for only a few seconds you see the girl that until four months before had literally hung the moon for you. And this glimpse punctuates your relationship, the way you know that any strokes painted after the last one would only be to the work's detriment. Over.

An elbow pokes into my ribs. "What up?" says Dylan. He scratches his cheek. Prestor John debates the set list.

"I think I just saw Tara, or some girl that looks like her."

"I'm doubting it was her."

"Even so...I know...kind of fucks with me."

High heels of various lengths keep descending the staircase. Most of these heels come to stiletto points. The owners sport everything from skirts and fishnet stockings to fraying denim jeans. When did all of the girls start wearing heels?

"I'm going to go find Andrew," says Dylan. He stands up and walks toward the merchandise table.

A few minutes pass while I space out. The band stands up and leaves, and I'm left on the couch staring at the back of the staircase watching shoes. To my left, on the other side of the sagging yarn, some guy says, "What're you down for, man? It's a rock show." He rotates his hand as if to say *come on*.

"No reason. Just spacing," I say.

"You look bummed out. It's cool; you should be soaring. What band are you in?"

"I'm not in one. I'm just with Prestor John."

"V.I.P. Rockin." He gives me a thumbs up and then extends his hand. "Ed Pineyurn."

"Taylor Matts."

"How do you know the band?" Ed Pineyurn appears to be in his forties. His complexion: a heavy acrylic mixed with sand. His peppered-grey hair grows out from a shave. His t-shirt looks worn and his denim shorts fray in places. I can hear Scott sound checking his vocal mic.

"I went to the U with the one of the singers."

"All right, you went to the U. Put her there," he holds his hand out for me to slap.

I slap his hand and say, "I'm going to check this band out, so I'll catch up to you later."

"Until later."

I walk under a brick arch and find Dylan and Andrew standing at the edge of the growing crowd. People gather in front of the stage as it becomes apparent the band is about to play. I tell Dylan and Andrew about Ed Pineyurn, and we joke about still being stuck here when we're in our forties: no women, no children, and still cheering stupid bands by another two generations of failures. Dylan wonders why some aging hipsters have that gung-ho optimism. Is there a point where one is able to give up on life and then revel in bucking social constructs? With an affected accent Andrew says that the whole social construct is a fallacy, man. That what is genuinely necessary and what is perceived as necessary are two entirely different things. Take deodorant. Humans do not naturally stink. If a human stunk, he or she would have trouble reproducing. Evolution would have solved that. What's happened in the last century is capitalism. Capitalism has found a way to market and profit from creating a false hygienic necessity. Deodorants, anti-perspirants, colognes...these products constitute several hundred-million-dollar markets. The average day-laborer works extra hours every week to be able to afford these quote unquote necessary products....

Andrew keeps on with this diatribe in his affected accent long after Dylan and I ignore him. At the point when I think Andrew's gesticulations and lamentations are attracting attention, the band starts to play. There are four members in Rejected Ego. Both Scott and a guy with a three-inch mowhawk play guitar and scream. A short, squat guy with unkempt hair and a priest's collar beats the drums. The bassist looks like a skater and has a shaved head. Rejected Ego's intensity surprises me; their melodic notes rip into my ear. I turn to say something to Dylan, but he jumps behind Andrew and grabs fistfuls of Andrew's shirt near the shoulders. A moment later the two plow through the crowd until they join the circle of people moshing around the beam in the middle of the crowd.

I look around the crowd. Many of the girls have permanently inked their baggage onto full-sleeve tattoos. They forsake the opportunity to marry a doctor or businessman. So they dye their hair blond and streak it with black. And they smoke cigarettes and may have diseases, and most can tell you every item they have eaten for the last week. And they're frail and they're pale and somehow still busty, and cradled in boyfriends' arms. They all have large eyes and aggressive hair. Regardless of the lighting it's never hard to see their lips.

I know Tara is in here, but I don't know how to look for her. I don't know if she's accessorized to match a new boyfriend or is still the same, or even what her same is with me not a part of it. But in between the groups and couples and single people, just out of sight, I keep seeing familiar colors and curves. The shapes match.

From behind me I feel hands clamp my shoulders, and I expect to start throttling through the crowd of people in front of me. Instead the hands begin squeezing and releasing. Out of the corner of my eye I realize it isn't Dylan's hands on my shoulders, but Ed's forty-year old, masculine hands massaging up my neck and shoulders. Then he works over the surface of my back.

I take stock of the situation. I stand in a dank basement watching angry students and hipsters exercise melodies while this guy I don't know kneads his hands up and down my back in a surprisingly knowledgeable fashion. I'm glad it's dark. About the point I go to wipe the ridiculous smile off my face, I feel two flat pats on the back, and Ed walks past me throwing a thumbs up. I nod.

Rejected Ego plays two more songs while I wander through the crowd to the back near the abandoned bar and then even over to the area by the entrance with the merchandise table. The homeless kid with glasses asks me if I would like to buy one of the Crimethink books, but I walk away before we can discuss it.

When the lights come back on, I find Dylan and Andrew covered in sweat and recounting pit stories. I tell them about Ed's massage, and Dylan asks me why I didn't just punch the guy.

"I didn't know if the guy was hitting on me or just trying to cheer me up," I say.

"It would be great," says Andrew, "to not have to drop you off on the way home if you plan on going home with a piece of anus tonight."

"It's more than you'll get," I say trying to stretch my shoulders in a way that will erase the massage.

Dylan asks, "Should we head to the bathroom?" and taps the flask that I know he has in his pocket.

We make our back to one of the worst restrooms in the city. One panel of mirror is missing and the other is so scratched and covered in graffiti it struggles to reflect. Most of the faucets lack handles and the urinals lack activation mechanisms and are full of piss so yellow it's almost brown, but I have to guess at the color because of the strange purple lighting. Wet paper towel stripes across the ancient black and white tiles, which is strange, because at the end of the rows of sinks is one of the recyclable *cloth* towel dispensers, with the face of the dispenser torn off and most of the cloth towel in a soiled pile on the floor below it.

We're not alone in the bathroom, but Dylan pulls out the flask and asks, "Who'd like the honors?"

Andrew looks at me, but I hesitate, afraid that if I smell the stale urine while swallowing straight gin, I might chum all over the place. Dylan shrugs and pulls a hard gulp. I take the flask next and find that because I'm trying not to breathe through my nose, it's actually easier to drink the gin. We pass the flask until it's empty, and Dylan re-pockets it. We return from the bathroom to an even larger sum of people, and it occurs to me that Tara *really* could be here. The three of us run into several people we know while Prestor John sets up their gear and sound-check. I really didn't think there was enough in those sips to get me drunk, but I find myself so damn…*convivial*.

When the main lights go dark again Dylan asks me if I'm going to head up front.

"I can't now. I'll puke."

"You're not going to puke, pussy."

"I'll get in there later."

With the opening drum crashes both Dylan and Andrew rally away from me into the crowd mass. This time listening to the music I bob my head and pump my fist and back-up the choruses. I'm almost entirely in that little place of my own when again I feel the heavy hands working over my shoulders. Ed's hands on my shoulders keep me from bouncing to the music and fuck up my rhythm, so I tear away from him and flee into the anonymity of the crowd. I push into the multitude of backs and arms; eventually, they give and for one second

I stumble free of them—before Dylan crashes into me from the side and throws me in the direction the circle moves. I crash into the wall of bodies and hands and am thrown forward again.

I put each foot in front of the other and let the rhythm dictate pace. The edge of the circle reaches out and throws me back in line when I lean on it. And the song slows until all that's left is Ian quieting a single note. Andrew is next to me so I smile and laugh at him, and he smiles. Prestor John is a moody space-rock band and the next song is one of their brooding ballads. I love these songs, because Ian will croon in that sexy sad way sounding hurt and meek and simultaneously like he will use you and spit you out. The song opens with Ian strumming a slow minor chord that drains all of the bouncing and skipping from the circle and the crowd is struck contemplative, calmly waiting. And when Ian opens his mouth I'm already aware that we'll never get past this song, and our dreams of rockstar futures are simultaneously fulfilled and destroyed in the same instant, and everything, literally everything you have to offer has culminated in this one brilliant expression, a collapsing soul's crescendo, and simply...it's not enough, not only not enough, but will never be enough, because that peak marked the highest point of expression and some souls were just born with more, and yours isn't one of them. When Ian says the word "chalice" his tongue plays with it like a razor that cuts him mute. The frustration in failure won't die quietly, and you are primed early by Dave's single edgy and heavily filtered guitar notes cutting across the simple melody, so that when they start stringing together lines of their own, they're angry lines. They're the lines you wish you could say to ex-loves in the heat of the moment; the lines you've been editing and saving for an absent parent; or lines for a parent you sometimes felt you needed to reach across and shake by the shoulders saying, "See me. SEE ME." They're the lines that explain to a critical brother the futility of picking up a paintbrush. They're the lines Vincent saw as he turned the pistol to himself. The lines Ray Johnson's splashing made. Lines that won't get recorded.

In this basement everyone's face is slick and dripping. The same people that punch you will pick you up. You'd have to throw pebbles into the acrylic to capture the cragginess of the walls and people's skin are various mixes of yellow ochre and raw sienna over thick gesso. Mars black lips smile and hair is either titanium or ivory. The entire bottom half would be ground in the clothing and it would be all ivory or burnt umber. A technician would throw in highlights of alizarin crimson and ultramarine. But separating individuals would be ludicrous. At the base we're one throbbing body, individual cells of the same swelling and contracting muscle. Even that is off; maybe you're looking at charred trunks in a dense forest. There would have to be the eyes and you cannot record the eyes, because in a painting eyes are always looking somewhere and in the real world they aren't. Some of the eyes point to the ceiling, some are closed. In front of the musicians eyes watch fingers short-working; they watch the strings so the musicians won't have to. An accurate portrayal of the scene won't capture the eyes. At a real rock show they're useless. Ian stares at tits. I notice a spot of blood on the t-shirt in front of me.

How do you paint flavors? A show sweat collecting in trickles from dripping hairlines, flung drips in the face from locks of mop wet hair, and the sponging of a t-shirt back from the guy in front of you who is always a head taller. And it all tastes like your sweat, which when you sweat and pant enough rejuvenates you. Above me in the swirl, I catch a glimpse of a glowing ember, something in softened cadmium, both yellow and red. I think of God's eye winking. Mitchell hits his crashes.

# BLAKE (SEPTEMBER 20, 2005)

We are not making any money today in room service. The hotel is between conventions and the occupancy is low. I have taken three small orders in two hours. Theodore wants to wait until after dinner before he cuts me, so in the meantime, I hang out in the cashier's booth pestering Sonja. She sits on the stool reading an issue of *Utne*, while I interrupt her.

"So, Sonja, you have a small, self-sufficient lesbian community in Wyoming made up of women who really want to take the radical-cultural feminist initiative at face value and establish a mini-society without men. They live on a large communally-owned property with their property taxes paid for by an endowment. The women never have to leave the compound and are entirely self-reliant."

Sonja turns from her magazine and says without much enthusiasm, "It sounds like a wonderful place. Now do you mind if I sit here and read this...."

"Wait a sec," I say. "I'm getting to the problem. The issue is the women's paradise is very near the location where grey wolves are being reintroduced to the wild. The problem is that the grey wolves keep killing the women's livestock, and some of the women have shot at the wolves. This has resulted in a huge controversy. The question is, when you receive donation mailers from both the women's society and the wildlife society, which one will you donate to?"

I sit back in my chair with a big grin, but Sonja shakes her head and goes back to reading her *Utne*. I pick up one of the phones and call Annette.

When she answers I say, "What up, Dolls?" and I notice Sonja smirk into her magazine.

"Hello, Doll," she replies.

"How's work?" I ask. I turn my body away from Sonja.

"Eh," she says. "I took the kids to The Jungle Bunny for pizza."

"It's not seriously called that," I say.

"What?"

"The Jungle Bunny?" I slur my words a little bit hoping Sonja will not hear.

"Yeah...it's like Chuckie Cheese's. One of those places with little kids' rides and singing robot—"

"But a...." I don't say anything.

"What?"

"...nothing. Was it fun?"

"It was alright. I'm just watching TV right now. The kids are sleeping. I'll wake them up for dinner pretty soon. Hailey Jade is sitting next to me watching TV. She can hold her head up now, it's really cute."

"Sounds fun. Did you call the doctor?" We went to the doctor, because Annette was worried she had contracted thrush from the kids. The doctor ran some tests, and she was supposed to call for the results.

"No, not yet."

"Dolls, you've got to call them soon. They probably close at five."

"This is why you called, isn't it? God. I would love it, if just once you could call and not try and tell me what to do."

"I didn't call to tell you that. I just wanted to see what you were up to."

"And you what, wanted to check up on me? Call me later."

The phone clicks. Sonja is still reading her magazine. I say, "OK, well call me back when you find out," to the dial tone.

I hang up the phone. If she took care of things, I wouldn't have to worry about them. Wouldn't have them constantly running through my mind, clouding everything I should be thinking about.

My writing has been horrible this last week. My mute characters stare out of the page with blank expressions. Every sentence dies before the period. Last night I met with Nate and he told me about a piece he was adding where this kid tries to be a knight in contemporary society. He wants to live by the code of chivalry and courtly love. Only he's a Dungeons and Dragons nerd living in a dormitory at college. His roommate is more popular than him: the kind of guy who highlights his hair and has jeans that are faded in the right places. And the knight is sort of an outcast. He grows nervous whenever they bring alcohol into the dorm room and is such a disagreeable human that nobody likes him. There is this really beautiful girl who lives down the hall with curly, blond "locks." Nate is actually calling them "locks" in the story. She's the clichéd flirty-type girl with ogling eyes that always smiles and talks to everyone, even the outcast knight. Because of her attention, the knight falls in love with her, stalking around the campus at night to protect maidens' safe passage from their cars to their dorms, going on nightly quests to discover relics no average student acknowledges, etc.

The knight is not really courageous enough to accost anyone, and assuming he was, anyone he confronted, being approached by a five-foot four, mop-haired kid with glasses and a white t-shirt with a red cross colored in marker on it, would hardly be intimidated even in the dark college dorm parking lot at three in the morning. So the knight watches these people from a distance, unaware of the fact that they can see his vague outline behind trees and in bushes. Rumors begin spreading about a stalker, and the knight who hears these rumors becomes determined to catch this stalker, sort of his overall quest, and he begins spending more time watching at night. This only fires the rumors.

Until a rainy night he sees his highlighted roommate step out of a car with the blond-locked Mary. The roommate has an arm around the Mary, and pauses for a minute to attempt to kiss her, and she pushes against his chest saying, "No, not now." This transgression incites our knight, who is hiding behind a thick fir-tree trunk. With his wet red-cross t-shirt clinging to his emaciated chest and glasses fogged, yells "Leave her alone." The sudden intrusion from the dark startles the Mary who screams, and the roommate realizing he's found the stalker charges toward the tree trunk, tackles the knight and tears off his red-cross t-shirt. In a dramatic flash of lightning, the highlighted victor sitting astride the tackled knight discovers that the stalker is his nerdy, generally-disliked roommate who has been causing all of the dorm girls to be unnecessarily tense. In retribution he beats up the knight and pulls off his pants to humiliate him. The story ends with our knight crouched down in a rain puddle, shirtless, in his soggy briefs, crying into his knees while upstairs his roommate, after bragging about discovering the stalker, sleeps with the Mary and when about to cum slips a finger into her butt.

## BLAKE (NOVEMBER 10, 2005)

We become creative when there is nothing else to do. I follow Dirk across the sixth floor and then into the service hall behind the guest elevators. In the middle of the hall we sit on the floor and drink the mini bottles of Jack Daniel's Dirk stole ten minutes ago. We haven't had an order for over a half hour. Theodore won't let anyone go home because he's afraid we'll get a rush after the First Step Organization dinner lets out.

Dirk asks, "Have you made any money?"

"I've got two dollars to my name."

"This sucks," says Dirk. He finishes the last of his first bottle and begins opening a second.

"I still can't believe George is back with his parents." I say this to avoid talking about my relationship. I don't want to have any more conversations about how much better off I am.

Dirk looks at me and probably wonders why I'm talking about George. He says, "Yeah...you think your place sucks...at least it's yours."

"But what the hell happened? He used to bring his

wife flowers like almost every day. Hell, he'd prune bouquets together and combine them to make them look nicer." I fight to the end of the little bottle, and Dirk tosses me another one.

"She never liked this job. He's like thirty-five years old and works in room service. His wife is in real estate. She's a cunt."

I think about the kind of people that work with my mom. They all embody the salesman image; they lease foreign cars and buy nice suits. Everything is purchased on credit. It is the great American fallacy. Janitors making seven dollars an hour can have a greater net worth than a six figure salesman.

"What about his kid?"

"He stays with his mom, but George takes him every morning."

I try to imagine what it is like for George to move back home with his parents. George, the future me. All I can think about is all of the times Annette and I fought, because I had to stay late at the hotel. This whole conversation has nothing to do with George, and I think Dirk understands that. I stick an empty mini bottle in my pocket to discretely dispose later. "So that's the new American family?"

"Cheers," says Dirk and toasts his mini bottle.

# BLAKE (NOVEMBER 11, 2005)

All afternoon I sipped box Franzia blush and lay across my couchless cushions, my bed now that Annette took the mattresses, while the sun cut through my blinds bringing warmth to my face. I stared at the ceiling while waves of nirvana flushed through me again and again. I don't remember what, specifically, I thought, but I generally decided life was worth a giant hug, and after striking low, I was bound to float back to the top. Now with the sun gone and my head throbbing, I think about that idyllic stretch of time like a family camping trip spent in the redwoods or on a water-skiing boat. In my kitchen I weigh drinking water straight out of my tap from a moderately clean glass versus finishing the opened Natural Light can in my fridge. I wish I remember when I put the opened Natty-Light in the fridge.

Nate and Charly are on their way over to pick me up for a Kilby party. The night feels too dark for eight o'clock. When they arrive I'm hunkered down in my tight black jeans, a t-shirt Nate made in high school graphics class that reads, "skater then less than," a wool sweater vest, and my Pumas with no socks.

I say, "Hey-y-y. I'm not wearing socks."

We stop at the liquor store on the way to the party. The liquor store is peopled mostly with mid-lifers looking for a way to kill last week's memory, but there are a few weekend warriors like us humping the American dream. Charly heads toward the bourbons, and I follow Nate to the malt liquors. I'm only semi-decided on matching Nate's forty of St. Ides when I see the doctor, Vox, is on sale for twenty bucks.

"I thought you were trying to save money now that you have to cover all the rent," says Nate watching me rub my fingers up and down the rivets of the Vox glass bottle.

"Dr. Vox is *therapy:* you can't get that for twenty bucks," I say.

Back in the Bronco Charly asks me wasn't I trying to save money? I say no.

"So who is playing tonight?" I ask.

"Don't know. Scott called and said they might play a few songs, but it's a private party not a show. Hence the alcohol," says Nate.

Charly says, "Crack the Vox and let me take a swig."

"Kill that, bra. Therapy ain't in session, yet." Charly shrugs and mumbles something. In the front seat I can tell he's fumbling with his bottle of Ancient Age. "Put in the Rejected CD," I tell Nate.

"I just made this rap mix, like today," says Charly. He takes a swig of the Age.

"And it's one hundred percent fantastic, but we're going to a Rejected Ego show, so...."

"Listen, Super Fan: my ride. Plus we're going to hear Rejected in like twenty minutes. Don't get your panties in a bunch."

"Point made, bro," says Nate. "We're almost to Kilby anyway."

Charly says, "Served." I watch him take a second quick pull.

The doctor sits on the floorboard in a paper bag, nestled between my feet. I begin picking at the plastic seal with my thumbnail. From the radio, a sped-up vocal track says, "THOSE TEARS WILL CRY...AND WASH." Charly and Nate talk about Tyler leaving a hollowed apple on the countertop stinking of resin. Annette will come back for more of her things. I know it, but I don't know when. Nate asks why Tyler even needed the apple, the guy has more glass tubing in his room than a chemist. I get through the plastic seal and wrench the bottle out of the bag. As I twist off the cap Charly says, "That was my apple." The fruity whiff of the bottle hits my nose while the rim touches my lips. I should drink it slowly, but instead I throw the Vox back and take a strong pull. The warmth is vibrant and glittery, hits my stomach and spreads. I think of those commercial cartoon diagrams illustrating the effectiveness of medication. I exhale and breathe fire like a god.

"I thought you were waiting," says Charly's eyes in the rear-view.

"The Doctor is in."

On Seventh South cars have begun parking on the street. This is a good sign. Charly parks just outside the alley that is Kilby Court, and we walk up. Various scenesters graze in herds up and down the alley. Kilby Court is a tiny strip of asphalt lined with the entrances to warehouses interspersed with residential homes. Walking down the alley the various facades make me think of movie sets. One cinder-block building has an industrial garage door with a bright doorlight and an office-style door next to it; the tudor house next door has a stone-lined garden with fresh soil. In the back of the alley, the venue owner has converted a garage into an all-ages venue. The lot to the side of the garage has a fire pit. All other details about the venue are variable. The restroom is usually in a separate artist's studio across the street. During the Olympics they could sell beer there as well. Once there was a second stage in the artist's studio. Once there was an arcade in Kilby Court, once a photography exhibit. With little parking in the alley itself, parking on Seventh South becomes mandatory. But this is only when people show up. When the scene isn't a bust. When it's worth being here.

I like to think Charly, Nate, and I walk down the alley like we own it. Like our walk would be worth watching in slow motion with a really poppy soundtrack. Hey-y-y, I'm not wearing socks. There are clusters of people around various cars. Nate nods to some kid he knows that I don't. Most people are huddled near their cars, sharing cheap beers and cigarettes. Because it's a private party, most of the people look familiar, everyone having to be on the guest list to attend.

Charly says, "You're going to let me pull on that vodka."

"When you finish your bourbon," I say. I turn to Nate and say, "Is there going to be a mélange of available coochy nougat at this motherfucka or what?"

"How long have you been waiting to say that?"

"I wrote it on napkin at work," I say.

Charly unscrews the Age and takes a pull. He winces and says, "I'm good with issues and tattoos."

"You're not good with anything," says Nate.

I say to him, "You're good with tissues and baboons."

"Hey!" Charly pauses. "I want some of that vodka."

At the entrance, Scott from Rejected Ego has put us on the list, "Nate Adams +2." At regular Kilby Court shows there is a cover and no alcohol. Because it's a private party, we enter with bottles in hand. Nate talks to Scott and the rest of the band in the garage while Charly and I hang out around the fire pit. Across from us, a couple of guys and a girl talk amongst themselves. I vaguely recognize them. Others line the peripheral.

"There's good money in it and the guys I work for are idiots. If they can do it, I'll make a killing," says Charly.

"My mom's a realtor and works with lenders all the time," I say.

"I should have lunch with your mom," he says.

"Not worth it. She hasn't worked much lately." I let my eyes glaze over in the flames.

"You're not working very hard with the doctor," says Charly. "I've almost tapped the Age." He shakes the little bottle in front of me.

I look up and then to the bottle. I take two good swallows before I bring it down. With a good exhale the vodka tastes like little more than fruit juice. "Your bottle's not a fifth."

Nate comes out of the garage and walks up to us. "They're almost set." The sound checking inside the garage rattles its sheet metal walls and ceiling.

"Fuck it," says Charly, "let's go get some beer."

"My Ide's almost tapped," says Nate.

"We're not going to watch them play?" I ask.

"We've heard them before," says Nate. I'm heavier standing than I was sitting down. Back down the alley the clusters of people are distractions. Some loud asshole yells, "raise the roof." In front of the house with the stone garden an old Hemingway-looking man sits in a group of ugly twenty-somethings. A group of possibly attractive ladies walks past, and I fake pause as if to turn and follow them. I catch back up to Nate and Charly with a big smile on my face.

"Don't think you're ready," says Nate.

Charly slaps me on the back and says, "Come on. He was born ready."

"I'm like Ivan the Conqueror." I giggle. "But I'm going to be like Vlad the Impaler."

"I hate you," says Charly. "Can we leave him in the car?" he asks Nate.

The gas station is a flickering of fluorescence, and I don't leave the car. I put in the Rejected Ego CD and turn to the soul ripping song. Before the song wrecks me, Nate and Charly climb back in the Bronco talking over the song. We don't get to that one part I want to hear by the time we're back at the alley. I want to hear that part. The alley is different on our second stroll through. More people congregate right in the middle of the street. I take sweet pulls on the Vox and impress myself. Charly keeps the cube of Keystones in his left hand and an open beer in his right. Nate crosses his arms when he talks to people. Charly laughs with a guy named Chuck and then pretends to uppercut him Mortal Kombat-style. This girl named Monica that Nate has been working on tells this guy with long hair across from me that I am writing a novel. Monica says Nate and I are the smartest guys she knows and the guy nods.

"You ever read Delillo?" he asks.

"Pretty stuck on Rowling." I can't tell if my contacts are working. My world is squinty.

"I read everything Delillo writes," he says.

I try to say *Ratner's Star,* but he doesn't hear me over the people. He goes on about some screenplay and *Cosmopolis.* I whisper a secret to Dr. Vox and try to find

Charly and Nate. The alley is packed full of people. I see this girl, Michelle, who I've always thought was hot standing around beer-weighted older guys.

I point to Long Hair in front of me and say, "De-Little-O," and leave him standing there. Heading toward Michelle, Charly floats into my peripheral, and I slink close behind him and steel a beer out of the cube. Continuing on I hear, "But you've still got vodka." I stop and pull the Keystone tab with the hand holding the Vox. Right before I get up to the group of people with Michelle, I take this huge swig of beer.

I spit all the beer out on my chest and yell, "Shit's like a J-Lo video."

The various retards around her say, "I like this guy." "Yee-haw."

I didn't get any of them with the beer.

"What up, baby?"

"You are pretty thrown," she says.

"I'm a rockstar. How are ya?"

But before she answers, Nate throws his arm around my shoulders and says, "Hello, Michelle," with a Velveeta accent. Then he leads me back across the alley.

"I was putting out the vibe," I say.

"You look like shit," he says.

"Aside from...the sort of music video thing going on in my head...utterly fantastic."

"You mind if I pull a quick session with the doctor."

I clench my fingers tight around the bottle's neck and stare hard. Two blinks undo it, and I shake my head. "Yeah," I say, "totally. Go for it."

Nate brings the bottle back and takes it to the halfway mark. Ten dollar's worth of liquor gone. Nate wipes his mouth with his wrist and says, "Woop."

I thumb the cork back into the hole.

"How are you doing?" he asks.

"What do I know? It's like I don't think about it, and it rushes back and kicks me when I'm not looking. My writing is lost, my girl...I have to sleep on my couch cushions, since she took her mattresses back. I have an empty bed frame.

"You could buy new mattresses," he says.

"There are conversations to be had that haven't been had. All of these words that should have been said that maybe never existed. I don't know. It's mutual, you know? I don't want her to go, but all we do is make each other miserable."

"What has she said?" he asks.

"I don't know. We've only talked like twice. I forget things as soon as they're said. The behavior is a symptom of deeper problems in the relationship. I need to grow up and be a man. Get a real job."

"What? Does she think this will last forever?"

"I never remember our fights. We don't fight...in language. I don't feel good." I shake my head. I run over to this cyclone fence surrounding industrial rubber barrels.

# TAYLOR (NOVEMBER 11, 2005)

When we first hear the gut-emptying gags and coughs Andrew says, "Sounds like the kind of person I would know." I assess the type of people Andrew knows (almost all of whom I know) and completely disagree.

I shrug and so we walk over toward this cyclone fence where, sure enough Andrew's right. My hunched-over brother sprays umber-ish liquid out of his nose and mouth. He holds a liquor bottle by the neck with one hand and the cyclone fence with the other. Near his shoes is a blue plastic cup that with the asphalt, dirt, fence, and plastic barrels...just...*looks* perfect.

"What up, man?" I say.

Blake looks up from the ground at me with water-glazed eyes and says, "Taylor?"

"What in the heck you doing here?"

"Just asked you the same thing," he says.

I look at Andrew and shrug. "No you didn't."

Blake pulls himself up and turns to us. The hue of his face has shifted a few degrees greener than normal. The front of his t-shirt is all wet beneath his sweater vest, and he holds a liquor bottle in his left hand. He tries to regain his posture, stick-like legs in tight jeans, and smiles. He puts both of his fists on his hips and then points to me and says, "Hey, I'm not wearing socks."

I look down and don't think he is.

"How'd you find out about the party?" I say.

"Nate knows Rejected Ego. Who you with?"

"Prestor John. Band that played after Rejected Ego. I had art with the lead singer. I didn't see you in there?"

"Bro, I didn't watch the bands. I was in therapy." He shakes the bottle he is holding.

"You're pretty messed up about Annette," I say. I like vivisecting bullshit-cool.

"What is that?" asks Andrew.

Blake displays the bottle in both of his hands and says, "Boys, let me introduce you to the doctor." The glass bottle has a circular crater pattern and displays the word VOX.

"Vodka," says Andrew.

There is about a third of the bottle left.

"Did you drive?" I ask.

"Surely, you don't think…" but when he catches my eye he says, "Nah, *cap-ee-tawn*. Charly drove."

Andrew reaches for the bottle and says, "Let me have some."

Blake ignores him, and I say, "Aren't you cold?" I don't see my breath, but I think I could. Andrew is in his maroon parka and I have an old Hanes hoodie over a sweater and a couple of t-shirts.

"Just one drink," says Andrew. Blake gives the bottle to Andrew.

Blake picks at the front of his old t-shirt, "I hadn't really thought about it."

Andrew takes a pull from the bottle. When he goes to

hand the bottle to me, Blake says, "Hey there."

"I'm pretty sure, you've had enough," I say.

Blake shakes his head. Even his head shake is drunk.

"Save the rest for tomorrow," I say.

"Killing the bottle tonight. You don't cut on therapy."

"Calm down, Mom. If you're killing this, I'm drinking some." I take the fifth and swallow as much as I can. Nate Adams walks over. He is dressed in tight black jeans, probably Levi's, and a Misfits sweatshirt.

"S'up, bitches? I see you found the Champion," he says and pats Blake on the back.

Blake puts his hands together and gives himself cheers.

"How's it going, Nate?"

"Your ex is here," he says.

Andrew looks at me. "What a bitch. She can't come to our parties."

Nate shrugs. Blake reaches out for his vodka, so I lift it again and swallow. Vox tastes surprisingly fruity.

"I'm sure she's with some snowboard friends," I say.

"They looked like tools, but shit, everyone is here," Nate says looking up and down the alley. He turns back to us, smiles, raises his eyebrows and pats his hands on his chest.

"She doesn't get our scene," Andrew says to me. "I'm going to go tell that slut off." I try to tell him not to, but Andrew disappears behind a group of people.

"Ok…" says Nate. "I didn't think there was still such a sour edge—"

"There's not," I say shaking my head. "Andrew's just being dramatic."

"He can be annoying," says Blake. Nate and I both look at him.

"Well," Nate uses both of his hands to point to Blake and me, "now that you're both single you can give the ladies the Twin Matts Attack."

Blake sighs and looks at the ground shaking his head. I cringe.

"You're last name backwards is 'tame,' bitches," says Nate. He walks off with Blake following.

I call after them, "IT'S 'STAM.'"

I look up and down the alley at all of the groups laughing, spilling, and flirting. I'm still holding Blake's fifth. When I shake it in front of my face the clear fluid splashes back and forth in transparent waves. I pull the cork out and throw it on the ground. I drain the bottle in one mighty pull and then throw it over the fence, which causes a loud ruckus against the rubber barrels. People turn toward me in nearby groups, and I raise my arms up and yell, "GOAL," in my best soccer-announcer accent.

I don't let their looks register as I walk past them down the alley. It's a cold night and a lot of people wear sweatshirts and hoodies. Wool beanies cap most of the guys. It's cold. The alley is full of people, a large college contingent, way more than the tight designer jeans, vintage t-shirt, black-hair scene kids. It makes sense Tara is here. Groups of people sporting snowboard logos, sweatshirts, and beanies ground this scene. These girls have all done their hair, and I'm afraid to look at the wrong one.

I see Dylan talking to Ian by some of the other Prestor John guys near the house at the beginning of the alley that Ian and some of his friends used to rent. Everyone smokes and is holding a bottle of Coors Light. When I walk up to them I say to Ian, "You guys rocked out tonight."

"Thanks. It seemed like a good show. Could you hear my guitar though?"

"I heard it fine," I say. "This show was actually mixed

well. It didn't sound wall, and I could hear everyone."

"You could hear it, dude," says Dylan.

"The sound guy kept me low in the monitors. Just feel like I couldn't hear my guitar. I hate that."

"Did you know Tara is here?" I say to Dylan.

"I know your brother's here. I saw his friend Charly."

"Andrew and I ran into him...fucking Tara, though." I look at Ian and say, "The ex," and he nods and then hands me a beer bottle out of a case by his feet.

"Thanks," I say.

"What? Are you going to talk to her?" asks Dylan.

"I hope not," I say.

"How long were you guys together?" asks Ian.

"Three years."

"I had a girlfriend like that all through high school. I made a rule, I'm not doing high school again with a girlfriend," Ian says and then smiles.

Dylan points at Ian while looking at me and says, *"That* is funny."

"I just keep thinking I'm going to turn around, and all of sudden she'll be there and there'll be that horrible pause when I see her that's going to burn into my mind for the rest of my life: that it is *her,* and before I can even decide whether or not to say hello she will have noticed the look in my face and that pause, and it will be way too incredibly melodramatic. I hate that. I wish there was a way I could see her without having to look at her. It's that look that's going to get me."

"You watch too many movies," says Dylan. "You know what's going to happen? If you see her, *if,* you're going to think that she looks hot until you stop being a dink and realize that she's got too much make-up on...her hair's frizzy, and she's still an insane, crazy Mormon bitch who will wash you on the rocks again and again and again…."

"I get it."

"I'm not trying to be a dick, man. I really think she's a nice girl, but she's absolutely fucking crazy. I mean, we're all fucking *off,"* Dylan points toward Ian as an example and shrugs, "but she has huge deeply personal, spiritual issues that she doesn't know how to resolve, and I don't want to see you rack yourself over her."

Ian nods while taking a puff of his cigarette. Andrew comes up to us while lighting a cigarette.

"Jesus, if everyone's smoking, give me one," I tell him.

"I thought you quit," he says.

"I got so good at quitting I quit it," I say. Dylan gives me a sort of half smile. Andrew lights my cigarette. With my first inhale I feel my lungs tingle and a mini rush runs up and down my body. It feels like all of this pressure releases in my skull and pours down my spine. I feel really good for the first time tonight.

"Two and a half months wasted," says Dylan.

"Not wasted," I say. "Now I know how hard it is to quit." I pull the cigarette out of my mouth and wave it in a rainbow while humming the little tag song to The More You Know NBC public service announcements. Ian walks over to some of his band mates to talk to them.

"Did you find her?" I ask Andrew.

"No, but she's lucky I didn't. This scene is ours."

"What do you care?" asks Dylan.

"I'm just looking out for our boy."

"You should be trying to find a problem of your own."

"I'm working on it. I should give Nicole a call right now." Andrew slips his cell out of his pocket and flips it open.

"Now? You got her number three weeks ago. Your window has closed," I say.

"How come you didn't call her sooner?" asks Dylan. Andrew pushes a few buttons on his phone while examining the screen and then flips it shut.

"We were never doing anything. Besides the window hasn't closed anyway." I'm buzzing from the cigarette. Things appear slightly blurry, but I think my eyes might be tired or dry from the smoke.

"Jesus, you gotta go do some shit on your own, man. We can't baby step through everything," says Dylan.

"Just because you dated a girl like a year ago—"

"We were together for three years," I say. I finish the last of the cigarette and flick the end off before dropping the filter. "I need a beer," I say.

"There's a teener of Natty Light in the car," says Andrew.

"Should we bounce?" asks Dylan.

"This shit is kissed," I say. We say bye to the Prestor John kids and walk out to Andrew's car. Out of the ochre lit alley, the crowd of sienna and cadmium heads, the laughs and exchanges, the clink of glass, the scent of rain, a hint of blond....

In the corner of my parents' garage Andrew sits on one of my old skateboards flipping through a book about color origins intermittently sipping a beer. I have the overhead garage lights on (two strips of double barreled florescent white) plus two shadeless table lamps (hundred watt bulbs: one on a stepping stool behind me to the right, the other closer to my mom's Lexus flat on the ground) turned on attempting to contrast some of the fluorescence. It's stupid to try and paint at night under the fluorescence, but I don't have any options.

"Have you read this book?" Andrew asks.

"No. This light is killing me." I swirl dabs on my

palette.

"It's pretty cool stuff. Do they teach you how to make paint from pigment rocks and stuff?"

"No. We read about it and do some stuff with glazes, but mostly they're trying to teach you technique and composition."

I'm drunk. I actually noticed my double vision on the ride home. We were stopped at a stoplight, and I saw two flashing red-light hands. What's funny is that the hands were both crystal clear. It was as if the crosswalk signal was attempting to push away tardy pedestrians.

I drop my head down in my hand and listen to Andrew turn the page in his book. The handle of my paintbrush digs into my forehead, and my eyes close to keep out the florescent light. My mind sways back and forth; all of the little people in the Kilby alley go on with their conversations, ignoring the sway. I open my eyes and the light cuts through my eyelids like the birth of a star. I stare at the canvas, its ground, a sienna-leaning-to-yellow. I begin swiping at it with white paint in crisscrosses to imitate the pattern on the garage walls. My strokes are half-hearted and appear sloppy, because each stroke is too distinct. I slump back onto the stool and throw my head back in hands while waiting for the white paint to dry.

I want to say something to Andrew, but I can't think of anything. On the ground, underneath the stool, is a little Double Bubble wrapper. I pick it up and wonder where it came from. The yellow and blue with the round white font looks deliciously balanced and symmetrical. The order of colors and lines in the gum wrapper seduce me. Still holding the wrapper, I extend my hand in front of the full-length mirror next to my canvas. Taped in different places around the mirror are several eight-and-a-half-by-eleven digital images I photographed of myself. My idea was to create a collage of images of myself on top of my reflection. This would turn my reflection into a cubist work. I want to come across in the contrast between reflection and photograph.

I stand in front of the mirror and stick the wrapper right over my heart in the reflected me. Andrew watches me and says, "Nice. It's like a blossom in the button-hole."

"It's my heart," I say.

"Your heart has been chewed up and spit out? That's…subtle," Andrew says.

I start painting my full-figure: half-reflection, half-photograph. I spend an hour painting a combination of lines that mix the rolling curves of my reflected clothing and the sharp swathes of the collaged images.

I look at my canvas and I look at the mirror. Something hasn't worked. When I look at the palette I figure it out. The color variations are off. Instead of looking fragmented, my painting looks like a poorly lit amalgamation. It's all in these colors. These fucking fluorescent lights muted the colors, and at this point I'm going to have to repaint the entire damn figure somehow and sometime in natural light when I'm not at school or at work which takes tomorrow out and means I can wake up at the crack of dawn on Sunday and maybe try again. Maybe repaint everything I wrecked tonight with bad light and tricky eyes. I shouldn't have drunk so much, or put this off until now….

I throw my palette down and yell fuck. I grab the edge of the canvas and flip it off its easel. Andrew looks up from his book, his lanky arms propped at the elbows on his knees. I collapse onto the cold concrete and cry. This is the only thing I'm supposed to be good at. The only….

# TAYLOR (NOVEMBER 14, 2005)

The radio clicks on and I wake up staring at my blank ceiling, the light sconce off-center in my field of vision. There are two indentation lines in the ceiling's rough pattern. The lines appear to be caused by slightly sunken sections of the wood as opposed to imperfections in the paint, which I'm sure was applied by roller and wouldn't do that anyway. What matters more than the cause of the lines is their randomness and depth. A perfect randomness.

I reach for the remote control on the night table and turn off some soft pop song I don't recognize. Up until a few weeks ago I used to set my radio alarm to play whatever CD was in the player. First I set it to shuffle songs. I'd wake up and feel off for the rest of the day, and I realized that typically, I listen to CDs from the beginning straight through to the end. By waking up to a track in the middle of the CD it was like I woke up in the middle of a project I never started. I woke up depressed and was always late to work, because I didn't feel like moving. Now I wake up to 103.2 Soft Rock. Neutral.

I play one of my CDs and pull out my work clothes. All of the furniture in my bedroom (armoire, bed frame, and night tables) comes from my parents' first apartment and has basically been lugged through three different houses. It was always the guest room furniture until we downsized homes and then it became my brother's. When he moved out a year ago, after practically living *here* with Annette, I moved in. Mom even decided to buy me a new mattress considering the original was thirty years old. Now my sleep is a dream. I think that's how I used to trick Tara into sleeping over.

I still want sleep.

In the shower I forget whether I have washed my hair already so I wash it again. I put on a pair of khakis that probably need to be ironed and a severely lightened-ultramarine collared shirt. I also grab the brown corduroy jacket that used to be my dad's. No one is in the kitchen, but I skip breakfast anyway. My little white Sentra is frosted over pretty well but starts, and I sit for a moment waiting for the windshield to clear and kick myself for trying to quit smoking again. I hate driving without cigarettes. The easiest way to mark time in a car is to chop up the drive by how many cigarettes it takes. Chop up the entire day by the number of smoke breaks. I used to feel better when I smoked. I wasn't always so depressed.

I drive to work almost blindly trying to peer out of this little hole in the ice on the windshield. My defroster is on high and along the floorboards of my backseat is an ice scraper I ignore. My car ride is silent except for the defroster and when I talk to myself. Technically the Sentra has a car stereo, but no speakers, and I really see no point in buying some that will probably be stolen.

At work I park next to Andrew's Corolla. He's outside the employee door talking to Nicole and Samantha while they all take these deep inhales of what must be relieving cigarette puffs. Nicole works at the cashwrap with Andrew and me. She has curly blonde hair that hits the middle of her back and a decent body that nice tits really aide. She is a super friendly girl and if it wasn't for the facts that she is nineteen and a hippie, I might really be able to fall for her. Samantha, a more lithe body and sexier clothes, works in shelving, and I can't help staring at her gigantic lips whenever she talks. Although she smokes, she claims to be a devout Mormon. I try to flirt and tease her that I really know better. Andrew is ridiculously overdressed in a grey three-piece suit and fedora, which I know he laid out last night before he went to sleep. What makes his appearance perfect is that he is wearing black Converse All Stars and white socks.

"Sup, brother," says Andrew. The girls both smile. He says this like I'm going to stop and talk to them for a minute. Instead I give him a, "Yo," as I blow past the three of them and into the back of the store. Fucking smokers.

Stepping into the back of the store I hear a loud slap and see a Chinese star stuck into the side of a cardboard box. From around the corner, Bob walks up to the star and pulls it out having evidently stacked two boxes to better approximate a man's height.

"What up, bro?" says Bob. I walk over to the two boxes, and Bob walks back to where he had been standing.

"Won't Pam shit? You're probably hitting books," I say.

Bob pulls the star back and slaps it into the side of the box again. He laughs to himself with his Bob-laugh that almost screeches at its peak, the eruption coming from somewhere in the middle of his girth. Bob is about five foot five and at least two hundred and fifty pounds. He perms his hair into a fro and except for the fact that he is Caucasian looks like he would be right out of a Fat Albert cartoon.

"It's a plush box," meaning only stuffed animals inside, "besides she's busy on the floor anyway. I can't stand being awake this early."

"Why are you here this early?" I ask.

"The truck is dropping magazines off early. They called me like an hour ago." Bob pulls his Chinese star out of the box and walks over to the foldout card table. He picks up a plastic forty-four ounce soda cup and takes a drink.

"You've got to ignore phone calls from this place."

"I don't have caller ID."

"Might be a wise—" Andrew and the girls' entrance interrupts me.

"Too good to talk?" says Andrew.

"I'm not hanging around smokers when I'm trying to quit. It's bad enough."

"So?" Andrew says and shrugs.

Nicole looks at Andrew like he's an idiot and says, "I'm sorry. I didn't know you were quitting."

"I'm trying to," I say.

"Yeah. Big quitter at work in the morning, but when you're drunk at a party, it's all *I quit quitting*," says Andrew.

"Why do you want to quit?" asks Samantha.

"And maybe Yo-Yo Ma is the world's greatest cellist, but in all likelihood, when things all size-up and time swings its heavy scale back and forth several times, artistic achievement in performance will probably only be a footnote in the pages of cello history, whereas the musical aesthetic value of composition will lean far more heavily toward the innovators and personalities of the age," I say. Lines like that should amply punctuate any argument. Andrew, Nicole, and I stand behind the cashwrap while the early customers circle the shelves. I don't know why three cashiers had to open the store, but Mike, in his infinite wisdom, has probably started worrying about the shopping crunch that comes with Christmas.

"You think that the teen magazine, fame bullshit will be more valuable to time?" says Andrew. Nicole laughs.

"Obviously there is fame of varying degrees and types, but personality, perhaps. Or maybe the artist fills a particular social role. Like regardless of intention, society creates this character for the artist to be and that, in the eyes of history, is what the artist becomes. But our culture needs a face. Even anonymous figures of the past are pictured as that generic Greek bust. This is why that John Cage random chance artist aesthetic will never gain much popularity in our society. Or why Pollock becomes popular, because his actions are very intentional. He does not pretend that the quote unquote randomness of his work is anything other than his specific action."

"Why would he though?" Andrew walks back to his register as a woman approaches with some books. "I think you're confusing the aesthetic of chance operations pushed by someone like Cage with general abstraction. It's entirely different."

Nicole begins straightening the books that have been special ordered. She's not listening.

"Painting is dead," I say. Nicole turns from the books.

"I don't think that's true."

"If anything there are probably more people visiting museums than any time in history. There are more practicing painters—"

I interrupt Andrew, "But those are hobbies. Painting

as an aesthetic force in our society is gone. It doesn't matter." Andrew shakes his head. "What?" I ask.

"That has been said so many times in history. Every time art gets dull or repetitive some asshole tries to declare it is dead."

"Woah," says Nicole. Andrew's customer is gone, but that doesn't mean we are out of a manager's ear range. He catches himself and looks to the right and left.

"I didn't know you cared so adamantly."

"I don't, but you're making excuses to just sit back and do nothing. It's stupid. We should be pushing our craft. Instead we'll end up at a bar tonight talking about how art is dead."

"It's too early in the morning for this." A man in his thirties steps up to the line. "Good afternoon, sir." I need a cigarette. As if reading my mind, Andrew steps around the cashwrap and says he's taking a smoke break. Nicole says she's in. "Did you have trouble finding anything?" This mindless repetition takes me through to lunch. The guy buys two pop sci-fi books. They match his ponytail, but I shouldn't make fun of him, because at least he's cordial. I don't hope for more than that.

An hour later I'm spacing out, staring at the magazine aisles when Bob comes around the corner. "Did you finish with the shipment already?"

"Ehh," he says and shrugs. Nicole helps an old lady who purchases a *Cosmopolitan*. I don't know where Andrew has wandered.

"What are you doing for lunch?"

"I'm splurging today. Want to come with me to Noodles?" Before I can answer him a mother with two little boys approaches the register. The littlest boy, maybe two years old, begins crying when the mother doesn't let him hand his own book to me.

When I get a breath I say, "Yeah, let's do Noodles."

Another hour-and-a-half ticks by. Andrew is yelled at by a woman because he won't offer her more store credit for her exchange. Bob pops up at the cashwrap and Pam lets me leave. In the parking lot Bob lights up a cigarette and offers me one.

"I can't believe you're trying to quit again," he says.

"I had a two month stretch. I'm sick of it."

"And this wouldn't have anything to do with a certain absent someone from your life?"

"Regardless of what it has to do with I'm quitting. It's a waste of money plus there is no reason to live addicted to something. I want to prove I can change."

"Yeah…that's not about a girl. Do you still talk to her?"

"For a while she was still calling me and sometimes I would answer, but it has been awhile now. I don't know what she's doing. I imagine she's on to the next man."

"That's the way it works. Love you one minute, leave you the next."

In the cool air the smoke from Bob's cigarette hangs in the air a few seconds longer. The end of the cigarette looks warm. "I don't understand why someone would keep calling someone they quote unquote love and not want to be with that person," I say.

"You make it sound like it's supposed to work out easily. Like shit's a puzzle with matching pieces." Bob exhales and forces a laugh at the same time. "Come on. From what you told me, this girl was Baggageville. What about people who get married, have kids, and it still doesn't work? They end up divorced and still in love and unable to live together. This shit you're going through is just the tip of the iceberg."

I'm quiet for the last few steps before Noodles and

then I ask, "Do you think Tara misses me?" I open the door to Noodles and Company for Bob.

"Hell I don't even know her, but do you really think that's going to stop her from getting on some other dude tonight?"

Bob orders a full pesto plate and a large order of macaroni and cheese. I order a small plate of spaghetti, and Bob calls me a pussy. We take our numbers and sit at an open table near two big windows in the corner. There are no clouds, but the light outside still appears muted. Lunch-time traffic clogs the intersection on the corner and every-which-way drivers scramble to stop and make turns and pass other cars. The restaurant is full of the same clientele as our bookstore: young families with too many children, groups of young wives with several discount store shopping bags, and single working-class men.

"What happened to the girl you were dating?" I ask Bob.

"You want to hear a story," he starts. "I dated Melanie for four years and then found out she was cheating on me. We used to fight all the time when we were alone. I mean, we could get along in public just fine, but the moment we got home it was like we were fired up. And most of the time I would blame it on her, like it was her heavy drinking at fault, and she was being a bitch. But I remember one time...we got home from having been out with her friends and before she started saying anything to me, I just laid into her about how she always gets wasted. And I remember thinking at the time, shit, I've picked this fight. It's an odd sensation."

I mumble yeah and nod. The waiter delivers our food. Bob forks his pasta in a distracted manner. It's not that he eats slowly, but that his heart isn't in the dishes in front of him. But maybe I'm making that up, because when he begins talking again there is a slight smile on his face.

"I guessed she was cheating on me early on...but you don't always let your mind accept things; you take your lover's word. Five or six months down the road I found her car parked outside of his house. You still feel like you've been punched below the belt just thinking about it." Bob takes a few more bites of food before he says anything else. He reaches into his pocket, pulls out the Chinese star, and puts it on the table. "Now I wait to one day put a hole in the dude's head."

Walking back from lunch, I stop and talk to Samantha, who is outside taking a smoke break. She offers me a cigarette and then tells me she thinks it's cool that I am quitting. Something about her attracts me in a good way. It's like when looking at her I can still be turned on, but I don't think about Tara at all. In her slender hips and narrow torso, I don't see those curves that simultaneously made me think of both Tara and WOMAN in some Renaissance sense. And, of course, her coloring is entirely different. Tara's fake blond hair and pale skin compared to Samantha's Mediterranean skin and dark eyes; you look at Samantha and expect a husky voice.

"I don't know. Dylan had talked about wanting to go to the Salt Flats this evening, but stuff is always up in the air until the time actually comes. What are you up to?" I ask.

"Some of my snowboard friends are having a party in the Aves. It will probably be lame. You get sick of sitting around, drinking with the same group of people every night." She flicks the burning part of her cigarette with her other hand and then flicks the butt away. Something in my head says, aw, what the hell.

"If you want to do something different you could

come with us. Driving out to the Salt Flats is like nothing else you could do in this country. I mean…it would be different."

It throws me a bit when she says, "Yeah, maybe I will."

"If you want to, cool. It's no big deal, though." Because I've basically just said, "fuck it" in my head, I add, "Just so it's not misinterpreted here, I definitely DON'T want to be your friend." I say this with a huge grin and try to convey how absolutely balls out I can be. Samantha laughs in an amused way with a slightly furrowed brow, and we both walk back inside.

A few hours later Andrew, Nicole, and I have a pretty decent line of customers. A woman in a business suit on a cell phone tosses a few books on my counter. She doesn't make eye contact so I start ringing them up without speaking to her. I love these faux movers-and-shakers types. It's all about Tony Robbins and investment books for their living room bookshelf. The phone is to show that she has a lot going on, even though she is shopping for books at three P.M. on a Monday afternoon. Everything: the suit, the phone, the hair-sprayed haircut straight out of the Eighties, is a front. I fear my late thirties.

I tell the woman her total, and she hands me a credit card while still chatting on her phone. Only after I hand her the receipt and a pen does she hang up. She picks up the receipt and looks at it.

"You didn't put on my teachers' discount," she says.

"I'm sorry. Do you have your teachers' discount card?"

"That's what I just said," she says as she begins fumbling through her purse.

I realize she wants me to void the transaction and refund the books, and then begin the process all over again re-ringing everything. There is a long line of customers and both Andrew and Nicole are busy. I have to call Pam on the phone and wait for her to show up with her manager's code. The woman finds her teacher's card and hands it to me. It reads Jennifer Bentley, Lyndon Johnson Elementary School.

"Ma'am, are the books you're buying for classroom use?" I ask.

"What difference does that make?"

"The discount only works for books that are being purchased for classroom use."

"Well, these are being purchased for classroom use." For some reason I doubt the elementary school kids are going to benefit much from *How to Retire Rich,* but it isn't my call. I pick up the phone and page Pam to the cashwrap.

"What are you doing?" asks the woman.

"I have to page my manager in order to cancel the order so that I can discount it and re-ring it."

We stand there uncomfortably staring at each other. The line of customers is long, and a gentleman in a trench coat taps on his books in agitation. The woman stares at me, but there is nothing else I can do. When Pam shows up, the woman complains about my lack of service. Pam stands up for me and hassles the woman about using the teacher's discount for non-classroom-use books. The woman, now frustrated almost to tears, receives her discount and then leaves.

After our P.M. replacements show up, Andrew and I make our way to the back of the store. I stop Samantha and ask her again if she wants to come with us.

"You won't regret it," says Andrew.

"That sounds like one of the opening lines of a horror movie," she says to him.

"Don't be lame," says Andrew.

Samantha opens her mouth in faux shock, and I say, "Hey, we don't need to go that far. If you want to come, you should come."

"Call me this evening." She writes her number down on a piece of paper. She walks out the employee exit.

"You see that?" I turn back to Andrew. "I got some digits."

"You should fuck that," he says.

Dylan, Courtney, Andrew, and I sit in my basement watching a *Simpson's* DVD.

"You should call that girl," Dylan says to me, "I want to take off." Dylan lies on my couch with his head in Courtney's lap. Andrew flips through an old issue of *Rolling Stone* while sitting in my lounge chair.

"I can't believe you asked Samantha to come with us," says Andrew.

"Why?"

"To start with, she already has a boyfriend."

"She never told me about a boyfriend," I say.

"Who cares if she has a boyfriend?" says Dylan. "Every girl has a boyfriend." He smiles at Courtney, who rubbing his hair gives it a tug. "Oww," says Dylan.

"Maybe she is unhappy with her boyfriend," says Courtney.

"Goo. I don't know that I want to get in the middle of that."

"She might just use you to make her boyfriend jealous," says Andrew. He laughs, shakes his head, and looks back at his magazine.

"Again, you're being a little girl about this," says Dylan. "If she has yet to mention a boyfriend to you and is willing to hang out, who cares if she has a boyfriend or not? This is all just drama you haven't gotten to yet...unless there's something else?"

"I get what you're saying," I look at Dylan and then the others.

"She's a tease, bro. Are you going to get all bent out of shape?"

My phone rings. I don't need this headache from everyone. At work next time I see Samantha I can pretend I forgot to call her, and it is that much cooler. Dylan reaches behind himself and takes the ringer off the hook and throws it over the table to me.

"Jesus," I say as the phone cord knocks over an empty Mountain Dew can and knocks a pen off the table.

"Hello?" I hear someone say through the phone.

"Hello?" I say into the phone.

"What was that?" A female voice.

"Sorry, Dylan threw the phone at me and knocked a bunch of shit over." On the couch Dylan makes a retard face and gestures that I'm a jerk-off. Andrew stares at me.

The voice on the phone laughs and then says, "Well, are you going to pick me up or should I head over to your house?"

"Samantha? Hey, I wasn't even sure you were coming."

"I want to. It sounds fun. You want me to head over to your place?" I look around at the mess in my basement.

"We'll come and get you. Where do you live?" Courtney raises her eyebrows as if to say "job well done." Dylan has a smile, and I can tell by the way Andrew concentrates on his magazine that he is jealous.

When we pick up Samantha, Andrew makes like he is going to get out of the car as well, but I say, "Don't worry. I got it, bro." Samantha's parents own a large white house with Corinthian columns. When I ring the doorbell, I worry somebody in her family will answer, but they don't, and she slips right out. She looks cute in tight black jeans and a black long-sleeve sweatshirt with a zipper and appears much shorter in her white Pumas. Petite almost.

We pick up Samantha and make our way out of Salt Lake on I-80 West. The moon illuminates grey clouds as they cut in front of it. It's a bit darker and colder than our usual trips to the desert.

"Dylan," I call to him over the Doors playing on the radio, "you don't think we have to worry about the salt flats being all muddy right now?"

He turns the radio volume down. "I doubt it. There hasn't been any rain for a while. It's been an Indian Summer."

"We could always hit up 'Dover if it's too wet to walk out in the flats," says Andrew.

"That is a bad idea," says Samantha. She sits in the back between Andrew and me.

"Why?" I ask.

"I hate Wendover. It's so depressing."

"I spent last Easter in Wendover," I say. And because of Samantha's look I say, "With my brother and mom...my dad was working so my mom didn't want to have to cook. She likes video poker."

A minute later Andrew says, "We won't go to Wendover."

"Relax. It's bone dry out there," says Dylan. "I promise."

I don't really know how he can promise, but it's not worth making an issue over right now.

We tell stories to kill time. I want to tell a story about

Memory Grove, but I don't know how to leave Tara out of the story. I don't know how to gesso her out of my life. It can be a long drive out to the salt flats, and the first stretch is the worst. I wait for that rest stop that's at the top of the valley. Eventually the Tree of Utah. But that's right near the end. It takes a while to get there....

Samantha tells us about betting on street races. She says that one time her friend ended up in the hospital when he was hit by a tire that a racing car threw.

Andrew tells everyone about the time I tried to win two free tickets to a comedy performance by telling a joke in front of some students in the Union's basement. Everyone who told a joke was supposed to receive two free tickets, but I didn't get anything.

Samantha tells us she wants to go to law school after college.

Courtney says that every girl has tried to pee standing up at least once. Samantha agrees.

Dylan says that the entire genre of country music is awful.

We reach the last long straightaway before Wendover. The salt flats stretch for miles either way cropped by the mountains in front and behind us. Even the mountains part as one heads north or south into the desert. When we drive past the Tree of Utah Samantha asks, "Have you guys ever gotten out of the car here and gone to see that up close?"
"Of course. We've written on it," I say. I remember

stopping at it once at 5:30 A.M. on a Sunday morning with Andrew, Dylan, and Nathan on our way to Wendover. The sky was already starting to lighten, but the sun hadn't risen. I remember walking up to the huge abstract statue of a tree and trying to figure out why the artist had painted it the colors he chose. The cool pastels make the giant balls, or fruit I guess, look like decorated Easter eggs. The stripes make the whole thing appear that much gaudier. The sculpture was made by some rich outsider artist. As if by creating the Spiral Jetty, Robert Smithson had opened up the blank canvas of Utah for every asshole with money.

When Dylan gets to the right mile marker, he drives off the road and for a second I worry the car will sink into a salt water sludge, but the ground holds. He drives a few seconds more and then kills the engine maybe twenty yards from the road.

"Everybody out," he says.

"You park right here?" asks Samantha.

"Why not?" I ask.

"We're like right next to the road. What if someone sees the car and steals it while we're out in the desert?"

"It's one in the morning," I say, "who's going to see the car in the dark? More to the point, who's going to pull off the interstate to check out a crappy-looking car parked off the road that may or may not have owners nearby?"

We all walk north. In the distance I can see the vague outline of the small ridge cut into the salt flats that runs at an acute angle to the road. The air is brisk for walking out in the desert, and the sound of the air makes a white noise that covers the sounds of the passing cars even at this short of a distance. It isn't windy, but there is a breeze. Near the car our feet make dry footprints in the salty crust. Because I am ahead of the others, I take the first step into the salty sludge. I stop and swear trying to shake the muck off of my shoe.

"God, don't walk here," I say hopping with one foot up.

"It must have rained," says Dylan. He crouches down and touches the two-inch-deep layer of salt frosting.

"Should we go back?" I ask.

No one says anything for a minute. Everyone stands still, except for Dylan who crouches, still touching the ground with his hand. Looking into the distance, the sludge has a perfectly still, smooth surface that reflects the night sky. The reflection eliminates the horizon line, so it is almost as if we stand on the edge of space.

When Dylan finally stands up he says, "We can walk barefoot."

"What? No," I moan.

Dylan has already begun untying his shoes, so Courtney does as well.

"Is it cold?" asks Andrew.

"Not really," says Dylan. He leaves his shoes and socks in a little pile and rolls up his pant legs. He takes a few test steps in the sludge and then says, "It's fine."

"Come on," Courtney says and joins Dylan. As they take their first few steps, their footprints leave soft indentations that look like strange floating divots.

Andrew takes his shoes off, so I turn to Samantha and ask, "What do you think?"

"I don't want to ruin my shoes," she says and bends to untie them. I shrug and do the same. When I step into the sludge barefoot I realize that Dylan lied: it is really cold. It is also soft and squishy and my toes sink individually into each footstep. With a few more steps we all appear as if we are shooting through space with little footprint asteroid-trails behind us.

"What do you guys want to do?" asks Dylan. "Do you guys want to split up, or walk alone for a bit...."

Interstate 80 is little more than a flowing line of lights. Other than the sound of our words and steps the wind is the only thing I hear. Clouds dim the moonlight and reflect below us so it appears that we walk among them. Samantha stands next to me, but is hardly more than a silhouette in her black clothes.

"You want to go get lost in the desert alone?" I ask.

"You're not afraid of the dark?" Andrew asks me.

He is smiling at me. I can tell by his tone.

"I don't want to walk alone," says Samantha. "That's creepy."

"Actually, I'm not afraid of the dark," I say. "You go off alone, if you want to get all mystical." I once looked Satan in the eyes during the hallucinations of a horrible acid trip. The prospect of walking alone into some non-dimensional space feels a bit like stepping straight into the recesses of my head.

"Fine. We'll split from here. We can meet back at the car in...what? An hour-and-a-half?" says Dylan. "Just follow the highway lights back to the car."

Courtney and Dylan walk north, but to the left towards the mountains at a western angle. Andrew walks directly north, and Samantha and I walk slightly to the east. With the light this dim and the constant sound of the wind, we seem to be alone after only a few minutes of walking. In this darkness though, we might be only two hundred yards away from Dylan or Andrew. It's hard to tell.

"What do you think?" I ask Samantha.

"It's the desert," she says.

"Wait a few minutes. I-80 is still close. Once we get far

enough out, it will only look like a vague glow in one direction. It will be way more surreal."

"I was hoping the stars would be out."

"We kind of have the cloud-thing going on, and the reflection is cool. Last time we came the stars were amazing. I mean, they are stars, like when you go camping, but the sky seems even bigger, because there are no trees out here."

We walk a few more minutes in silence. Vaguely parallel to our path is a short ridge in the salt. We decide to walk over to it. I stumble on a clod of dirt at its base, and we skulk up it and shimmy over the top. The ridge is probably only eight or nine feet high and runs in a straight line out of our visibility. I tell Samantha that it must be manmade, but I don't know why it would be. From on top of the ridge looking toward I-80 the darkness seems rounder.

We follow the ridge for a while, and I start thinking about the darkness. There was a period of time after my acid trip when I used to be able to see it. Like rather than darkness as an absence, I used to see darkness as a substance. And I could manipulate it. It was a fuzzy glowing energy that I could turn navel orange or morph into bruised-skin green. The dark was easy to change into the various yellows and blues of healing skin. Or the original night of my trip when I saw things in electric glowing whites, purples, and greens. The colors vibrated and flowed through whatever I saw as if it was a charged current.

I feel the tingling moving up my back like a shiver. "Have you ever done acid?" I ask.

"No, just pot and ecstasy. One time I got really drunk at this party and the next day my friends told me I had tried coke, but I don't believe them."

"I think you would remember...for sure. But I don't know; I've never tried it. Anyway, I was just thinking about this bad trip I had one time. It was the worst night of my life. I can't ever really describe why except that at one point I was lying in bed with my hand in my mouth, and I realized that I could literally bite through my fingers if I wanted to. The crazy thing is that after, I didn't have what I would call flashbacks, but I did still remember certain things. Like I was somewhat haunted by them. It had to do with the darkness. Being in the dark freaked me out, because I was afraid of what my mind could do. It makes insanity a scary thing. Artists, you know, that's their thing. I mean, I'm not saying they have to go crazy to be great or cutting edge, but...they've got to be able to see the world a little bit differently." Samantha doesn't say anything, but sort of nods as she watches the ground while we walk. I've been watching the ground, too, to keep an eye on my footing, and I wonder why we even come out to these places, go on a hike, if all we're going to look at is the ground two feet in front of us. I stop walking. It's stupid not to look at this, to see this. There is a thin line of silently moving traffic behind us that connects the dark globs of earth at the edge of our vision. Out into the flats to the north, the sky and ground merge into each other. With the moon darkened behind clouds and the sludge reflecting the sky there is no horizon line. No sense of depth. It's like you stare into eternity. Into a void. What a black hole must look like. Anything could come out of that blackness. That void. A collapsed mind. The ultimate progenitor. And so God stared into the darkness and there was the universe. And every artist must stare into the darkness, and I've ruined my ability to do it. To look naively, no fear of the void. Ignorant of what comes out. But I have seen what came out. And why don't you paint it? You can't paint experience. Experience is the past and you can only paint in the present. Even now looking down, because I feel the vibrations and the tingling, and I don't dare look out.

Then I look around and realize Samantha is gone. There's no way she could have missed that I'd stopped walking. This means she decided to walk on without me.

"Samantha," I call out softly. She doesn't respond. I consider calling out louder, but in the darkness I can't see who might also hear me. The darkness could swallow me up. God knows. I have no desire to clench up and have to be found in the morning because I paralyzed myself with fear. To move. I start running forward. Further into the desert. Yes, intentional. But possibly toward Samantha. Trying to chase her footprints. And it's not too cold to run. It feels nice. I can see the freeway off to my right. I'm not lost. Just running in the desert late in the night. Could something be trying to catch up to me? Someone? The chills. These are not good thoughts. I'm psyching myself out. Freaking myself out. I've done this before. I was fine. No. I almost bit through my hand. I never would have bitten through my hand. I am fine now. Was fine. Nothing's wrong. No Samantha. This is stupid. I need to stop running. Lungs starting to burn. Whether I want to (I don't care) or not, I'm going to have to stop soon. Let whatever it is catch-up. It's nothing.

My footsteps slow. I can't help that.

I stop running and catch my breath. Over the sound of the air blowing I hear my heavy breath. This is the foreground soundtrack to every horror movie. I need to stop doing this to myself. I breathe in; I breathe out. The stupid desert. I could swallow this darkness. Is this what happens when a woman leaves a man? He runs out alone in the desert to come back new? Was this what Jesus and

Moses were doing? There are stories I should know. I should be familiar with them for at least culture's sake. How long since we went to church with any regularity? I wonder if we ever went weekly. A lifetime ago. I don't think religion is something kids learn from churches. It comes early from parents' threats or later from life's. Tara knew all the stories, and thought God would still damn her. Believed in telling her Bishop everything. Her Bishop was a proctologist, lived three houses away. And this is God's way? Man was no different from any other. He had a wife and kids. He never tried getting drunk with his med school buddies? How else do you end up in proctology? Like he got into that field of medicine with no sense of greed? *You're not trying to be a better person.* I am a good person. Say it. Shook her head. Just say it. That's not—YOU CAN ADMIT IT. OK, I want you to come with me on Sunday. I fucking knew it…or maybe I said, so fucking predictable. Got in my car and left. Maybe there was more than that.

I sit down. My pants sink in the sludge and I can feel the moisture creep up my shirt. It's getting late. For some reason, sitting down makes me think the darkness is swallowing me. I'm too tired to be scared now. Or maybe, I want the darkness to take me. I lie down on the sludge floor and feel the sticky salt suck down my arms. The starless sky with grey shadows moving over and reflected below. Scorpions, spiders, and snakes. Even the jack rabbits look like they bite out here. I see myself sinking into a well of darkness, watch myself lowering away. But then I'm always back inside of me. Through these eyes? These eyes are what see. I am these eyes. When they open, when they close. Is there a difference in the dark? It's not like before. Now there's glowing blanketed grey moving; now there's not. What if I fell asleep in the desert? What in the fuck's a matter with you? If the dark doesn't scare me does that make me cured, different? No, because there's still the bugs. But in the wind you don't hear them. The wind blows and plays its own song....

It's the distant soft-calling of my name. I'm asleep. I sit up and uselessly try to brush salt sludge off of myself. The sky has gone from blue-black to grey-black. It is still night. I stand up. My eyes are sticky, and I rub my head. I call toward where my name is coming from and start walking back. In the grey Dylan appears.

"Where in the Hell have you been?" he asks.

"I fell asleep."

"In this muck?" he asks and lifts his foot. "You were supposed to meet us an hour ago. Samantha said you got weird and ran past her. That was like, a while ago."

"Yeah...."

We walk back to the car. Andrew and Courtney ask me where in the Hell I was. Samantha seems distant. I don't ask her why she ditched me; in fact, I start to wonder if she did ditch me. For most of the drive back we're quiet having left something of ourselves back in the desert.

# BLAKE (NOVEMBER 21, 2005)

In front of the television, little stacks of DVDs and CDs spread like a necropolis, reaching me at the couch where I lie prone and tune in and out of a movie. My front room smells like the cats' litter box. I look at the piece of paper in my hand and try to think. The piece of paper consists of the ripped corner of a credit card application. I have handwritten "Grocery List" across the top, but haven't added anything below it. Finally, I add the word "food" and the word "drink" below it.

Two hours pass in which I stumble around the room reshuffling piles of DVDs and moving dirty dishes around. At the end of the time, I still haven't emptied the cats' litter, cleaned up the floor, or even washed the dishes. My grocery list still only has four words.

I walk into the kitchen, and my phone rings. I answer it, but no one says anything. Usually, I try to hang up before the telemarketer can speak, but this time I hear the hollowness of a connected line and know that someone is on the phone not saying anything. I tell the person I can hear him. After a few more seconds I hang up. In my fridge sits a gallon of distilled water. I pour myself a glass, and the phone rings again. This time when no one says anything I tell Annette she could at least have the balls to say something. I tell her if she is going to be a slut, she ought to at least be a bitch, too. I drink a gulp of water and in the pause a voice says, "Sober soon. You will be called." The line clicks dead. It was a man's voice I didn't recognize, and I wonder if this is the guy Annette is fucking now. But what does that mean? You will be called? Is he calling me out and wants to fight? What is "sober soon"? I walk back to my couch and sit down. Luna stands from the arm on the far end of the couch and walks over to me. She wants to smell my water, but I keep her head away.

My phone rings again. I look at Luna for a second and then I walk over to it and pick up the receiver.

"Hello?" I say.

"Hey." I recognize Annette's voice.

"What in the hell are you doing having someone call me?"

"What are you talking about?" she asks.

"Like two minutes ago, someone calling me and making threats."

"I have no idea what you're talking about."

"Bullshit, you're such a liar—"

"I've been at work all morning—"

"And the guy you're fucking now couldn't possibly be trying to mess with me."

"Look if it's going to be like this, I've got to go."

"YEAH, WELL THEN HANG UP YOU COWARD. I'VE GOT SOMETHING SPECIAL FOR THE TWO OF YOU. I'M GOING TO CONK HIM OVER THE HEAD WITH A BAT AND THEN KNEEL ON HIS CHEST UNTIL HIS HEART

STOPS. YOU CAN'T STAY IN THIS TOWN YOU FUCKING BITCH. SALT LAKE IS NOT YOURS..." but the line has already been dead for some time.

# TAYLOR (NOVEMBER 16, 2005)

Andrew and I sit in the Desert Pub waiting for the waitress to bring us our lunch. The pub is almost empty and only one of eight pool tables is being used. We sip our respective steins, and Andrew screws together his pool cue.

"I don't have any idea what the fuck happened to me," I say half-glancing at the silent televisions playing ESPN.

"You freaked out in the desert, man. Big deal."

"Yeah, that's not normal. At least if I were drunk it would have made sense," I say. On the television screen a baseball pitcher throws a pitch and then gets hit by a line drive in the chest.

"I didn't know you didn't have any alcohol. Both Dylan and I brought our flasks. I think we just assumed you had as well. It was rad as crap drinking out there with the ground reflecting the sky," says Andrew. He stands and walks over to the nearest pool table and begins racking the balls.

The three of us bought matching flasks when our favorite antique store in Sugarhouse put up its liquidation sale sign. We would always visit the little Asian shopkeeper, whom we'd first met when we were fourteen and he sold us "paperweights" (brass knuckles and Chinese stars). Dylan and Andrew almost always carry their flasks with them, but I'm too lazy to keep mine filled.

"I didn't even think about alcohol," I say, "because I was too distracted by the fact that we were hanging out with Samantha."

"It might have helped if you were going to have some acid flashback. Do you want to break or do you want me to?"

"You break," I say and pick a pool cue off of the wall. "I didn't have an acid flashback. Not really. I've had one of those before and they're different." Andrew breaks the balls and gets in the 4-ball. I'm stripes. "This was more like the world was abandoning me. It was the weirdest thing, but it was suddenly like I wasn't going to exist anymore."

Andrew pockets one more solid, but misses the next shot. "You're up," he says. I circle the table and try to find something that is so easy I could accidentally make it in. "Well, none of us think you're any crazier, but you probably messed it up with Samantha."

I shank an easy shot at the 9-ball. "Samantha will probably talk to Nicole as well, so that's out of the question."

Andrew lines up his shot. "Not necessarily. Chicks like guys that are screwed up. I mean, not like Samantha who doesn't really want the artsy guy anyway, but Nicole might dig that. But there's no way she's going to like you over me," he says and smiles.

"I really think Samantha ditched me out in the desert," I say. "I mean, I don't know...I was kind of distracted being crazy, but I think she just kept walking and left me behind."

"Who knows? She probably did." Andrew knocks in a second ball, but misses his third. "This could really work out for you. Samantha thinks you're a freak and crazy, but Nicole wasn't there, so she'll probably just dig you because you are dangerous or damaged or something."

The waitress brings us our burgers. She's a little older than us and has the quick smile of someone who works for tips. Her eyes are a bright blue for a brunette, and they get round when she smiles. We tell her thank you and ask for another round of drinks.

"I think I should ask our waitress out," says Andrew. He smears ketchup on the veggie burger in front of him. I mirror his motions with mustard over a real burger.

"I think this chick's too old for us. Plus, she might be married."

"Did she have a ring?" He takes a bite of his burger.

"I never look for rings. I don't even know which hand they are supposed to be on." I put some ketchup on my burger. Highlights from a footbag competition play on the television. I remember sipa in junior high.

"It's the left hand, moron."

"Why would I know this?" I ask.

# TAYLOR (NOVEMBER 19, 2005)

I stare off into space at the bargain aisles in front of my counter. I need a job that pays more money. I spend all of my money on expensive art books. If I get a car insurance bill soon, I'm screwed. I see Samantha cross the center aisle halfway down the store. Since the salt flats we haven't spoken one-on-one. An old man brings a newspaper up to my register.

While ringing the old man up I see Bob come around one of the magazine racks. He nods so that I can tell he wants to say something as soon as the old man leaves. I nod back to him in the direction of the back room. When the old man walks away I ask Nicole if she can cover while I go talk to Bob for a second.

"You're not going to lunch yet, are you? I'm starving," she says.

"I'm going to talk to him for two seconds and then you can go. Is that cool?" She gives me the A-OK sign.

In the backroom Bob sits on a folding chair drinking Mountain Dew out of a fifty-two ounce refillable plastic mug.

"What up, man?" I say with a dirty South accent on man so it sounds like "main."

"This bookstore's a joke when no one's here. I have to strip and throw out twice as many magazines when no one buys anything. I think I'm going to go into the bathroom and take a nap this afternoon. I used to do that at Sherwin-Williams."

"You're my hero if you actually take a nap on the clock."

"Call me Superman, then. It's done." He takes a long drag on his straw. "What are you doing tonight? I'm spinning at a club in Holladay."

"Not uh. I'll go if I can say, 'I'm with the DJ,' to the door guy."

"I'll put you on the list. The club is in that strip mall next to Cantina on 39th South."

"The club is in a strip mall?"

Bob shrugs.

"Cool, man. I'll be there," I say and start to walk out of the backroom when Bob tells me to wait. He walks over to his backpack and takes a CD out.

"You've got to check this shit out," he says.

"What is it?" I ask and take the disc from him.

"Just some porn, bro."

"Oh...cool." I look at the blank disc in my hand and then back at Bob. "It's not...weird, is it?"

"No, no, no." Bob laughs. "It's nothing like that," he says. "You need to check it out, though."

"Alright, cool," I say softly. "Thanks."

# BLAKE (NOVEMBER 22, 2005)

I'm not sitting up today. Or at least if I could get through today without sitting up that would be a vast accomplishment. It won't be. I don't remember when I shaved last but it has been awhile. The days blur...the sense of timeline, when have I not been lying on this couch? Hirsute, a hermit, helpless, happenstance, happens, hastens, and then what? Holds? I finally learned the trick. The trick is that if the drinking never stops, the sickness never starts. But that's not true. You're still sick, but too drunk to care. Half asleep, half passed out...and then awake. This quake, this quake.

There is knocking on the door.

Standing is disorienting. Stepping over books in small piles all over the floor, the rubble of collapsed stacks of DVDs in front of the television. My body is numb; I feel my clay. Exhales are deflating. Luna is asleep on the kitchen floor, but where is Temple?

Nate smiles in the doorway. Somewhere Annette is fucking a new man. "You coming out today?" asks Nate.

"Somewhere Annette is fucking a new man."

"Probably not at 11:45 on a Tuesday." Nate walks inside past me. He turns, "Besides, maybe that turns you on." He walks over to the banana chair and sits down.

"You're fucked up."

"Somehow, coming from Boozy McDrinksalot that doesn't resonate like it should."

I walk over to the kitchen and step over Luna who hasn't stirred. I open the fridge.

"You want a beer?"

"Probably not...it's 11:45 on a Tuesday." Nate looks at me with a raised eyebrow. I walk back to the couch and lie down. I can't remember what movie is in the DVD player.

"You going to go get some job applications this afternoon?" Nate asks.

"Yeah, probably."

"I bet." I lie on the couch, and Nate sits there for a minute. The sun shines through the blinds in warm bars striping the couch cushion my feet lie across. I kick my socks off with my toes to feel the sun.

"Look, I don't want to have to be Captain Empowerment here, but you've got to get over this girl. For Christ's sake you weren't even happy while you were dating her. It's stupid."

"Thank you, for that seriously insightful, sage advice. It's a tidbit easier for someone who's got a girlfriend to say something like that."

"Oh, please. You think that is going to last? Last night at Urban Lounge I was trying to work it out with this new chick. That's how it is. You can't be expecting to find your soul mate every time you date someone," Nate says and shrugs.

"We were together three years."

"And it didn't work out. You guys were never meant

to be together anyway. You never had good times together. Everything was always one crisis after another."

Temple walks into the front room. We both look at her, and she looks at us. Then she walks over and starts licking Luna's head.

"I know you're right, but I just don't want to get up today. I'm feeling the weight, and it's not just about her...just in general," I say and stare at my dirty carpet.

"You should do some writing today. That will help."

I sigh. "I actually did some last night. Suffice to say I'm glad I can delete it faster than I can write it."

"It's part of the game. One saved line for every one hundred throwaway."

"What?" he asks.

"If I can write one hundred good pages by the time I'm thirty. You should read a book for every one page of writing you try to write."

I sense what is happening, but my mind won't solidify. It's so murky.

"I understand," I say. "I know all of this."

"I'm serious. Writing can save you. Make something of this."

My feet...they're so warm in the sun. I want to move them, brush them against each other. So heavy my legs aren't going to lift.

I lie on the couch. Nate isn't here. Luna lies on the couch's arm in the sunlight, light blinking off of her black fur. Outside a car pulls out of the parking lot. It's three P.M., and I'm hung over.

# BLAKE (NOVEMBER 23, 2005)

The night his car skidded and hit the wall.... The rain splattering on Jacob's windshield disrupted his view.... First there was the screech of brake pads being torn apart in a frenzy to stop the tires....

I hate this. I don't hate this, I need this. I need to pick up my CDs and alphabetize them again. No, I should sit and write. But I can't think. My mind is too distracted. I should put on some music to drown out the white noise in my head. But then I'll stop writing and start thinking about the music. Or remembering things. I need to stop thinking. Too much thinking. I need the music.

I walk over to my scattered pile of CDs on the floor. Mozart is good. Listening to Mozart makes you more intelligent. Write smart, right? I put the CD into the CD player and start piling my CDs into organized stacks. This is stupid. I set three stacks aside on top of the short bookcase against my wall.

I walk into my bedroom with all of my CD stands. I look at the CD stands with their rows, spotty from CDs being removed and not returned. They grin at me with gaps in their rows of teeth. I walk back into the front room and grab one of the three stacks from the bookcase. I take this into the bedroom. All I have to do is separate the CDs into alphabetical piles. I finish this, and I can do some writing with my mind clear. Not so distracted....

# TAYLOR (NOVEMBER 19, 2005)

I lie in my bed in the basement in the dark trying to blank my mental canvas of my job. My room is quiet, but I keep looking at the glowing digital letters on my clock. The burned CD that Bob gave me sits on my dresser. What the hell?

Standing now, I brush my hand over my face. I grab the CD and turn on my computer. There is only one randomly named file on the disc so I double click it. It takes two seconds for me to recognize Tara and three more seconds to be sure that it is her. On the screen she is shown from the shoulders up, apparently naked, laughing at someone off-screen.

The first you see of the man is a large erection that drops into the screen and slaps Tara in the forehead. Tara keeps her eyes closed, but opens her mouth and the erection slaps her in the head several more times. A large hand with a tattoo of a black heart on the top near the skin where the thumb and pointer finger meet holds the erection up so that Tara can start sucking on the balls. There is a masculine groan off-screen. Tara begins heavily fellating the erection, and the man's hands grab the sides of her head so that he can thrust deeper into her throat. When she gasps and pulls back, long strings of fluid connect her lips to the shaft, she takes a breath and starts laughing.

Tara's face looks more pale then I remember, but it's hard to tell for sure, since the lighting isn't very good. Her laugh has changed. The face fucking goes on a couple of more minutes and then she climbs on top of the guy and starts bouncing on his lap while facing him.

She looks strung out, and I can only imagine what bad habit has hooked her. The scene lasts ten more minutes and rips my stomach in two, but I can't look away. It ends with her exhausted, exhaling fucked-out gasps of breath and glazed eyes. I feel angry and sick and go sit on my toilet and jerk off. Then I watch the scene again.

# TAYLOR (APRIL 13, 2005)

In my parents' basement, Tara and I sit on the couch watching *Romeo and Juliet* with Leonardo DiCaprio and Claire Danes. Tara sits to my left, and I have my arm over her shoulder, which, since she is almost as tall as me, means she has to slump down in the couch. The light is off, and I look at her face in the glow of the television screen. The curve of her nose is pretty soft until it runs into the small bulb of the end of her nose.

"I want one of those guns," I say. Tara sighs. "What? Families always used to pass down the father's armor and sword. I want a big chrome handgun with my name on it."

"Guns are stupid, and if you get one I'm not going to hang out with you anymore," she says.

I smile and curl her up to me and say, "Oh, yeah?" We start kissing, and she pulls away to watch the movie.

"Did you see this movie in the movie theatre?" I ask.

"Yeah."

"Let me guess, it was on a date? When this came out everyone I knew took a girl to this movie and got action during it."

"That's really gross," she says half-distractedly watching the movie.

"Even I made out with a girl at this movie, and I never used to get any action."

Tara doesn't say anything, but I watch her face. I like this movie. I bought it, but that isn't why we're watching it now. I lean over and blow into Tara's ear. She shrugs her shoulder at me, so I blow into her ear again. She turns her face toward me. We're inches apart and with her face this close to mine it is all I can see. It amazes me her face looks so beautiful this close up.

"You're not going to let me watch this movie are you?"

I shake my head slowly. "No," I whisper. We begin kissing softly. I lightly brush my right hand over her sweatshirt. Our lips touch, but our mouths don't completely seal and our tongues barely touch tip to tip. When Tara exhales it turns me on, and I pull her to me with force. We seal our kisses more passionately. I think of that Rodin sculpture except that we're becoming more of a singular form. I wrap my legs around her legs and throw my right leg between hers. I'm more on top of her, and we begin gyrating into each other.

"We shouldn't do this," she says. "Your parents could walk downstairs."

In the dark her eyes don't have a particular color. "Why would my parents come down here?" I kiss her again, but she pulls her face away so I suck and lightly bite her ear lobe.

"We shouldn't though." I can tell that her body wants a whole lot more than she does. I slide my hand under her sweatshirt and then under her bra. With my fingertips I begin outlining her breasts and nipples. This makes her breathing heavy, and I try to swallow her breaths.

Through heavy breaths she says, "I don't think we should do this."

I keep touching her and then slide my hand down her pants. Her legs tense and squeeze together, but are sensitive to my touch and allow me to part them. "I don't think you mind," I say. I start massaging her folds, and she moans. She starts breathing really hard.

"Stop...please stop." She puts her hand on top of my wrist. After a few more minutes she sits back.

There are tears in her eyes. "I asked you to stop," she says.

"If you REALLY wanted me to, I would have," I say.

Tara stands up and walks over to the door and starts putting her shoes on.

"You're just taking off?" I ask.

She looks at me but won't say anything. Once her shoes are on, she leaves. I'm so pissed off I want to throw something across the room. On the television Mercutio says, "Tis only a scratch."

# TAYLOR (NOVEMBER 19, 2005)

I curl over my computer re-watching the Tara video, when I hear quick footsteps pad down the stairs. Andrew swings open the door, right as I close the file window, and I say maybe too quickly, "What up, man? What are you doing?"

Andrew looks at me and then a smile breaks across his face. "You were watching porn, man. I can tell."

"No, I was looking at art stuff," I say and shake my head. I begin shutting down the computer.

"Bullshit. Your face is all flushed. What were you watching? I want to see." Andrew walks over to the couch and sits down.

"Whatever," I say. "We're not hanging out watching porn together. That's a little too gay for me." I close my laptop and set it on my desk.

"You're such a faggot," Andrew says.

On the drive over to pick up Dylan I make Andrew play music that I have never heard. This is because I don't want to hear anything that reminds me of Tara, though trying to avoid music specifically because of Tara means that I am constantly thinking about her.

We call Dylan from the car, and he comes out wearing a synthetic, flashy club shirt that requires both Andrew and I to make fun of him. The rest of the drive to The Axum I keep thinking about Tara and wondering what in the hell happened. I wonder if it has to do with her father and his lung cancer. He's probably dead by now. Or maybe she changed after hanging out with her snowboard friends.

Few cars populate the strip mall parking lot in front of The Axum. The monster of a doorman finds my name on the guest list "plus one," so the three of us split the six-dollar cover for the third person. Once we are inside, Andrew complains about paying two dollars.

Inside, the club is dark and misters expel warm clouds. The laser lighting becomes visible shafts of light. I haven't seen a place like this since I turned eighteen and my friends and I went to dance clubs. Two overweight girls groove and gyrate on the dance floor. A few stray groups of people stand in clumps around different sections of the bench that runs along the walls of the club. There are a couple of stacked-stage sections to the dance floor, but these are empty. I tap Dylan on the shoulder and gesture over to the DJ booth in the corner, but he throws a thumb over his shoulder pointing at the bar. At first this frustrates me, because I know he's got a bourbon-filled flask stored on him, but I wave the two of them off and find Bob on my own.

Behind the turntables is a giant black man with a grown-out, nappy afro. Aside from a darker skin color, he resembles a super-sized Bob. Behind the booth, Bob roots through a case of records. I tap him on the shoulder.

"What up? You made it," he yells into my ear.

"Thanks for putting me on the list."

He looks around the club. "Not a lot of people yet. Still early. The promoter, Tony Granato, said Phoenix might come by. He's in town. Fucking Phoenix, man!"

I've heard of Phoenix. Some underground rapper. Why he would come to this club is beyond me.

I lean over to him. "I saw the video."

Bob lets the last record he was looking at slide into the case slowly. His body language becomes stiff.

"It's crazy, bro," he says. "I thought you should see that. There'd been rumors...I did some homework. If it's on the web, I can find it." He shrugs.

"There's no way that's fucking Tara."

"Look, man. I'd heard that after you guys broke up she started partying a lot with coke kids. One of them makes a ton of money selling snowboard stuff online. He's like the one who pays for everything. Anyway I think that's how they got the idea to start a porn site. That's where I got this clip. It's a demo clip."

"Ridiculous. We weren't even having sex. She's a virgin. How do you go from there to porn star?"

Bob shakes his head. "I'm not trying to pull one over on you. That's her. There's a whole website dedicated to them, Sluts in Zion. They even use that Salt Lake, Utah slogan thing, you know, S.L. U.T."

"What's the website?"

Bob looks at me for a beat. "Nah. I'm not going to do that. It'll drive you crazy. You need to get over this girl. I just wanted you to know."

"Fuck that," I say, but Dylan and Andrew come up to us. They say hi to Bob and pound fists.

"When are you spinning?" Dylan asks Bob.

"I'm on the wheels from eleven to twelve," yells Bob. Dylan and Andrew both nod. There is an uncomfortable moment of silence.

"Maybe I should grab a drink—" I yell.

"You guys should come see this. It's cool," interrupts Bob. Without another word he walks off and for one quick moment I wonder if we should follow him. I tail Andrew past a smattering of people and then through an unmarked door I hadn't noticed when we first entered the club. I follow them down a narrow hallway with masonite paneling lit only by red light bulbs that produce such a ridiculously ominous filter that I am tempted to laugh. There is a right turn and then a flight of stairs culminating in a final door whose opening produces soft yellow lighting.

We stand in a tiny room with a sofa, a coffee table, a matching sofa chair, and a small TV on a stand. All of the furniture is shabby and makes the room look like the set of a Seventies sitcom. There is even an obligatory rug underneath part of the chairs and the table. Bob walks around to the far side of the couch and retrieves a beer from a mini-fridge.

"They have a Green Room?" asks Andrew. Through the walls and ceiling we can hear the muffled sound of the base beats.

"Performers' Lounge," says Bob and spreads his arms out to gesture *all of this*. "Sit down, let's hang for a minute." Bob sits in the solitary chair while the three of us take the couch. The couch is upholstered in a corded material with a black, beige, white, and gold pattern reminding me of a similar couch my grandma owned.

"So do you already know what you're going to play tonight, or do you make it up as you go?" Andrew asks Bob.

"I like to know where I'm going to start. Once the records start spinning, I leave it up to what I feel and how the crowd is reacting—I mean, there's like cuts I've already practiced, like set links...but I don't plan like the whole hour. I don't know what kind of stuff Crispy Fingaz is going to play—you know, you don't want to double track. But I've always got options...it makes like the whole set seem more organic. Every set is different." Bob takes a pull from his bottle and then stares off across the table past us. I feel fidgety and crave a cigarette. I notice I am running my palms up and down my pant legs as if to smooth out a wrinkle that doesn't materialize. If I could make the rules about atmospheric light, I would make half of the room we are in orange because of the red light in the hallway.

"Yo, DJ B, you wouldn't have another beer in that fridge by chance?" I ask.

Bob winces. "I don't mean to seem like a cheap dick, but there's only like a twelver in here and all of the DJs are supposed to split it. I'll buy you—"

"No, no, don't worry about it," I say.

The door swings all the way open and a large Tongan man stands in the doorway with a shiny black parka and a hood. Under his right arm is a heavy-set, white redhead with freckles. She's wearing a black mini-skirt and a long-sleeved, striped cotton shirt.

"G'yo, Bobbo!" the Tongan yells to Bob.

"Sup, Doc?" The couple comes inside leading a train of short, white hip hop kids in gigantic clothing with overly made-up girlfriends.

In a moment the room has become a scene, and Andrew, Dylan, and I do not participate. For a second I look from conversation to conversation, but find no polite entry. Bob talks to Doc about a record he is excited to have found, and one of the hip hop kids tells the others a story of overdrinking and selling weed.

"You guys want to head back upstairs? I need a drink," I say.

"Let's cruise," says Andrew. I try to get Bob's attention as we stand, but he doesn't turn from the Tongan guy.

Stepping out of the red hallway back into the club proper has that same effect as when we first came in the club: there is a moment of darkness and then vague outlines begin to fix and one gets the sense that everything is being revealed. There are a few more people present than when we first went downstairs, maybe thirty total.

I walk straight for the bar line. For some reason the pasty, little bartender seems intent on ignoring me, and when I finally order my beer he raises his eyes as if I were ignoring him. I don't know where that comes from, but I tip him a dollar out of habit.

The beer in my hand relaxes me a little, and I don't feel the overwhelming urge to smoke that I was feeling back in the Performer's Lounge.

"I wish Bob was spinning right now," says Dylan. I know what he means. Standing on the sidelines of this mostly empty dance floor sipping our beer feels...stupid.

We take a seat on the bench along the wall of The Axum. Andrew quick-pours some bourbon from his flask into my glass. The Axum's crowd is a bust, maybe fifty people total, the bulk of which line the perimeter of the dance floor talking to each other in mini clicks. It reminds me of a middle school stomp. There are seven people dancing. Two of the hip hop kids from the Performer's Lounge try breakdancing moves.

"Cheers," I say, and Andrew, Dylan, and I clink glasses.

When Bob DJ's, he chooses unfamiliar cuts with vocal

styles that remind me of mid-Nineties, underground hip hop. Most people tend to prefer early Nineties hip hop, but I think Bob attempts to qualify the next chronological step. His music deals with skepticism rather than optimism.

I don't know. A resolute black guy walks by in what looks like a priest's collar.

We leave in the middle of Bob's set. I drop both of them off at Dylan's house, but decline to come in. I've become moody guy, since we left The Axum, but don't feel like explaining what is on my mind. I tell them I will call them tomorrow. I drive into the night.

Tara lived with her parents in Sandy, which is the first major suburb of southeast Salt Lake. The neighborhoods are safe, populated by middle and upper-middle class families. None of the home construction appears older than nineteen-seventy.

I hadn't driven around Sandy until I started dating Tara, but I find myself driving in that direction now. Twenty minutes later, I stare at her parents' house in the dark. It's a small, one-story, three-bedroom place. The second window to the right of the front door was Tara's room. I don't know if she still lives here. Her Altima isn't in the driveway, and it's one-thirty in the morning.

I want the house to tell me something that I don't think it can. Nor do I know exactly what it is, but the lawn is as manicured as ever. The shrubs are trimmed back. The walkway to the front door is clear of fallen leaves or cherries. I don't know what I expect.

Back in my basement I dig into the internet trying to find some clue or link to a website I don't want to believe exists. I hate searching through porn websites on my computer, it's like looking for a coconut-tasting pussy in a whorehouse. I can almost feel the spyware components harpooning tentacles into my browser.

Still, I can't find the site. I can't find the site, I can't find the clip I've already seen, I can't find a still of a clip with Tara's face. Every click can be six new girls I haven't already seen in Dali-esque splays and contortions, all taut larynxes and pooled napes. But there are consistencies. Specialty websites begin to feature the same actresses. The same blonde is gang banged in two different rooms. Two different men piss on the same brunette. In these niches I think I'll find Tara. Something in the web, maybe something about a snowboard chick or a Mormon having her throat raped.

Through the blinds, morning light begins creeping down the window well. I can't sleep, and I think I have wrecked my computer with viruses and spyware. The browser takes up to ten seconds per page. I haven't found one clue. I masturbated twice and feel hollow. I play the clip from the CD one more time. Tara's laughing face laughs through me.

# BLAKE (NOVEMBER 25, 2005)

Oh, delightful drunkyville. I stumble up from the couch over empty beer cans on my way to the fridge. Devoid of food, you still keep my beer frosty. I take two more cans back over to my couch. Early afternoon light cuts through my blinds. I prop myself against the arm of my couch in a perfect way that allows me to not have to sit up to drink. I begin laughing. My telephone rings, and I stand up to answer it.

"Ello?"

"Blake. We're cruising over to get you. Have some clothes on," says Nate.

"No, thank you. I'm perfectly happy with my telephone provider."

"Three minutes," says Nate and hangs up.

I plant my feet firmly on the ground before cocking my head back to finish my beer. When the can is empty, I raise it to the ceiling before slamming it into the garbage can. I hold my finger up. Why? Because I need clothes. This is a mandatory mission. The assignment's been assigned. Shirt and shorts. No. Too casual, maybe too cold. Man has strategy. Johnson, I'm giving you a raise. Jeans and a t-shirt, sweatshirt on top. You can't go wrong with denim. Not in my society.

Dressed, I walk back to the front room. Back to another little unopened beer. Hello, lonely little beer. I say this out loud to the beer can and prime it. I pop the top and call Luna a sleepyhead, because she is lying on the arm of the couchless cushions in front of the window. Temple watches me from across the room lying against the front door. I tell her no, although she's not really asking.

This calls for a party. I skip over to my CD player and play a CD that reminds me of skateboarding in the early Nineties. There is a knock at the door. "Who's that?" I ask Temple.

I let Charly and Nate inside. They look sober. "Party!" I say and toast no one with my beer.

"Yeah, it's two in the afternoon," says Nate.

"Best way to get past a Tuesday." I take a pull.

"It's Friday."

"It is Friday, isn't it? Huh." This surprises me. "Well...here's to getting past Tuesday."

"Nice save," says Nate. "You want to finish that beer, so we can take off?"

I look down at my hand. Oh, yeah. I walk over to my sink and pour the rest out. "I think I'm good."

In the Bronco driving away I ask, "Why are we out and about so early?"

"It's two o'clock," says Charly. "What do you care?"

"Special surprise," says Nate.

"Sweet! I know you guys think I'm a seventy-five year-old woman, but you don't have to throw me a surprise birthday party, promise," I say.

"Fuck off, or I'm going to shoot you," says Charly.

"We're going to the gun range," says Nate. He turns back to the backseat with a devilish grin to look at me. "This guy gave Charly free gun rental coupons and money for bullets if we were going to go to the gun range today."

"What guy?"

"This guy Charly knows."

"A friend of mine," says Charly.

"What does he care if we go shooting?"

"Dude, chill. I think they're referral coupons or something. He gets kick backs," says Nate.

"Why'd he give you money for bullets then?"

"You want to go shooting for free or not?" asks Charly.

Well....

We pull into a small parking lot on the west side of the valley. The gun store has the same blank walls and cheap shelving as a porno shop. All of the colors are dark wood and look laminate. The smell reminds me of cardboard. Along one wall are various large gun safes. The middle of the store has several aisles of gun and hunting accessories. Rifles line two of the walls, and handguns fill the glass countertop cases. There are three employees, two of whom look no older than we. The oldest employee talks to a nicely-dressed woman who appears to be in her forties. The gentleman pulls a ridiculously oversized rifle from the wall and breaks it so the woman can look at it. "And what kind of people buy guns like these?" she asks. Her question makes me wonder if she is a reporter.

I have to act sober. I doubt the employees will turn firearms and bullets over to a drunk. A gun range is no place for accidents.

We walk over to the counter and one of the younger employees asks us how we're doing. He is clean-shaven with short hair and wears a striped polo shirt. Charly gives him our coupons.

"That's fine. What would you like to try?" he asks.

"I'd like a .44 Magnum," says Charly. The guy behind the counter pulls out a few of the largest revolvers I've ever seen and sets them on the counter. Charly examines them and picks out one he likes.

"For you?" the employee asks Nate.

"A .38 Special, please." He hands Nate a revolver that looks like a detective's gun.

"And you?" I feel so dirty. No, sober.

"I've never shot a handgun. Do you have something small that I can get used to?"

"Like maybe something in the twenty-two range," he says.

He moves across the counter to take a few guns from the case when Charly interrupts him by telling me, "You don't want a twenty-two, bro. It's like a BB gun."

"Yeah, but just something to practice aiming with," I say.

"You can't pick a twenty-two unless you're wearing a freaking skirt."

"It is small," says Nate. The guy behind the counter laughs.

"Show him a nine millimeter," Charly says to the employee. He takes a handgun out of the case and sets it on the glass.

"This is a Glock 17," he says.

It looks like any other handgun I've seen. The employee takes it from me and clicks a button on the side of the handle that releases the clip. "It's got a ten bullet clip. Just face the bullets, the round-side with the round-side." He slides the clip back into the handgun, places one hand over the top and cocks it. "If you need to check the chamber, you can press this switch and it will uncock the gun. Just make sure you hold onto it while you slide it back, because it's not good to let the gun snap. She's ready to go."

"Is there a safety or anything?"

"With the Glocks, it is in the trigger themselves. See how it has a second trigger behind the first?" I don't understand how a gun can have a safety connected to the same place the gun is fired from, deactivated by the same action that the device should be serving to impede...I nod.

He provides us all with a box of bullets and then moves us down the counter where we sign in for the range. He takes our driver's licenses. We each take a pair of safety goggles and ear muffs. In the far corner of the store is a doorway that leads to the basement. The stairs are dark, but there is a bright room at the bottom with several stools. Big panels of glass line the wall so that one can watch the shooters. There is only one other person in the range. Charly taps on the ear muffs on his ears, and before I figure out what he means, this piercing explosion from the shooter in the range reminds me to protect my ears and eyes. I put on my ear muffs and the three of us walk through a set of double doors to the range.

We each take a separate stall and set our guns and bullets down. Charly hands me a few sheets of eight-and-a-half by eleven paper with targets on them. He clips one to my target clip and then shows me the switch to run the target out on a line away from me. I leave the target about three-quarters of the distance of the entire range. I can only push seven bullets into the clip, because my fingers are sweaty. I cock the gun and inhale....

# TAYLOR (NOVEMBER 20, 2005)

Dylan picks me up, and we go to a take-out Mexican restaurant. This restaurant is in the location of an old 50's burger stand. The design is apparent: adobe, southwestern clay motif laced with stainless steel trim. The doors have the pothole glass and are steel.

"What have you been up to today?" he asked me on the way over.

I had nothing to tell him. I slept until three P.M. with the lights off and my curtains closed. If I could I would have slept through the whole day. I tried to turn on my computer to websearch my ex-girlfriend's alleged porn site and instead wasn't able to get it operating, because I super-saturated the hard-drive with viruses last night during my all-night quest. So what have you been up to?

I cut up my cheese enchiladas, and Dylan scoops some carne asada fries into his mouth. The evening is early, and we have the entire lobby of the restaurant to ourselves (all three tables and two counters lining the walls). The employees laugh and talk to each other in Spanish back in the kitchen over a tinny stereo playing salsa music.

"I got to tell you something pretty fucked up, but you can't tell Andrew about it."

"What's up?"

"Yesterday, Bob gave me a disc at work that had an .mpg on it of Tara giving some guy a blowjob."

Dylan looks at me.

"I'm serious," I say.

"I know. Andrew found that clip a couple of weeks ago."

I must be making a face, because Dylan flinches. I stare over at the floor by the counter across from me.

"We didn't want you to find out...."

In the back of the restaurant I can hear the little stereo. The music has shifted from salsa to tango. The guy at the counter keeps walking back and forth between the back kitchen and his register.

"...but you'd probably take it wrong. Whether or not, we liked her, we wouldn't have given so much of a shit about you and her except that we knew she must have been hanging out with some pretty shitty people."

"You didn't tell me this when you first found out?" I ask. My stomach has that empty feeling, like when I see a patch of naked canvas in a finished painting.

"We didn't want you to try and contact her. It's not like she needs help or something. She is a different person now. Whatever choices she's made, she's not the same."

We are quiet for a minute. Someone pulls up to the drive-thru and orders a combination five and a six. He doesn't want anything to drink with that.

# ALBERT (DECEMBER 6, 2005)

At the office my door is closed, and I stand up from my desk, walk over to my bookshelf, and inspect my books. When I think I find the correct volume I pull the book to an angle by the top with my finger. I crouch close to the book, examine the title, shake my head, and let the book fall back into place. I then walk the length of the bookshelf twice pivoting on my heel, but shrug and walk back to my desk. I pick up the phone, punch a few numbers, and in another part of the office, a Lindsay stops typing on her computer and picks up the phone. She is maybe my son Blake's age and has pale skin, large eyes, and hair cut to her chin length. She nods twice, and we both hang up the phone.

I stand up from my desk and walk to my office door. I look back at my desk with both hesitation and almost a distinct sense that there is some reluctance to my having to leave it. My hand reaches for the knob and slowly turns it. Then I step outside the office in a quickhop. Sure enough, large and bearded Ed Morgan plows down the hall and stops right in front of me. For the imposing figure he presents (standing a foot over me, eyes darkened by heavy shadows in contrast with a pale cheeks and a stomach that practically reaches me when he stand three feet away), he smiles wide and gestures jovially pointing back into my office and then nodding and pointing toward me.

I smile back, shrugging, and then shake my head. And my mouth is moving to match how I hold my left hand near my face with pinky and thumb extended. I wave my hand past the rest of the cubicles outside of my office and then back to my office and pretend to shut an invisible door. Ed still smiles wide and stands with an exaggerated erect posture, hands in fists dug into the sides of his hips, and removes one to shake his pointer finger at me.

The words:

```
I hope that report is coming along.
The sooner you submit it, the sooner
you will receive the ATA credential,
and  we  can  begin  our  marketing
campaign.
```

I kick the ground with my foot, but then meet him again eye-to-eye and nod repetitively and point past him down the hall toward Lindsay's office. I circle around him, while constantly patting him on his large back and try to walk on down the hall. Ed reaches out, grabs me by the shoulder and spins me back toward him.

With his large arm over my back his smile grows thin and sharp. He waves his finger at me again, but this time slower, and I can feel the weight of every rise and fall of the point.

He releases me, and I speed off down the hall to Lindsay's office. From inside her office, one sees her typing away busily with headphones over her ears. Through the doorway, one sees me spin a circle and then pop my head into her office. I smile wide and wave. She smiles, pulls her headphones off, and waves me inside. I step into her office and point at her and then brush my hand past my face emphasizing the area around my eyes. Lindsay nods, holds her hands next to her head, and closes her eyes. But she shakes her head and then makes fists by her eyes, alternately twisting them back and forth. Her eyes are crinkled and her mouth is wide open. Then she gestures about rocking her baby and pacing back and forth. I nod and nod.

We continue like this for ten minutes until she opens her hand toward the bookshelf, and I raise my eyebrows in agreement. I pull the book from the shelf and look at it. Then shake it in front of her. I cradle the book and then point at her and then back out through her doorway. Lindsay nods and nods. I nod and nod, and she waves her hand down indicating her lack of concern.

I walk back to my office and along the way spot Ed over some cubicles. He smiles widely, and I smile in return. I close the door to my office. Very gently I set the book on my desk. I sigh. I walk back and forth in my office. My eyes outline the path my feet step, and my mouth opens and closes.

I sit down at my desk. I open my pencil drawer to where I keep the book I'm reading and some photographs. I pull out the photo of the neighborhood summer barbecue. Sitting next to Blake, I smile from the picnic table. He waves to the camera. Across from us and turning to smile are Karen and Taylor. To my right sit the Jacobs. Rich smiles with his daughter Julie sitting between us. His wife Charlotte sits next to Taylor, but does not look toward the camera. In the photo Julie smiles brightly from under a pink glitter crown.

I pick up the phone and dial the numbers for home.

# TAYLOR (NOVEMBER 25, 2005)

I watch the sounds of the footprints trace across my ceiling. I roll over. By the banging of the cupboard doors I can tell it is my mom walking around in the kitchen. It's eleven A.M. So right now. Right now would be a time for a cigarette. My stomach hurts and feels hollow: my body is asking it to support too much weight. The light through the window wells is the muted grey of winter. No vibrance in the light. This isn't the light that nourishes flowers. I need water. It's eleven A.M. You win, Mom. Or maybe breakfast. I want my stomach to go away.

I have class in three hours. I have to shower. My stomach needs to not hurt. I need water that won't nauseate me. I need water that is a four florin blue.

## KAREN (NOVEMBER 25, 2005)

The bottom line is that you can hardly be woken up by the garbage truck if you have been lying there half-awake for hours anyway, but I wish I hadn't opened my eyes now, the light searing my lids and making it that much more difficult to keep them closed when I finally now am trying to go to sleep to maybe finally rest to maybe finally dream a little dream finally. But why get excited against the odds that the phone won't ring, one of the kids won't come and ask me some nothing question I wished I won't have to answer? So bitter I should take one of those Yoga classes Luce invited me to, wonder where she is now. Could go to something where you post in an odd position, one foot up, downward dog something, and soft music plays and there are green house plants sprouting around the class. It'll be warm, and I'll fart, and we'll all fart together and unlike Albert's farts the group will smile shyly, but united, instead of frustrated and estranged.

Lying here, won't happen like this. Muscles are already cramping, and the room is too cold and the extra blanket fell off the bottom of the bed. Should buy a new one, too.

Mother's guilt. The edges fray and the seams loosen, but still softer than what I'm used to with these terrible rough throws and sheets with thread counts like bowling scores. Surprised my skin hasn't already broken into a rash. So dry. My throat is sore, so I'll get a glass of water.

The bathroom's a mess and the only shock worse than standing is the water going straight to my head and making it sway in that slow and dizzying rhythm like at the carnival on The Scrambler, and Jane wants me to sit next to Bob and between the heat and cotton candy. The temperature must have been in the Nineties at least, but California hot, not this desolate Utah heat, but the California version where beads of sweat break through your forehead and streak your make-up, and you're wearing too much then anyway, applied in the carnival bathroom, and the salt of the sweat burns your eyes and you have to dab carefully or you look like your abusive husband has had a go, or you are, trying to make life work on the wrong side of Oakland and that's what you deserve says Andy, step father. Simply eating the wrong type of food in this sun and heat will tip your stomach and rock it like that swaying pirate ship, so you run on empty and keep hassling the angry kids behind the food counters for cups of water, they'll pass to you, but not without some comment about you maybe meeting them once the park slows and the lights are burning, maybe say nine-thirty? So when Jane's humping Mike's arm and he says we should go on the Scrambler, Jane becomes hoppy and excited like Daddy won her the big, stuffed bunny, and I play it cooler with Bob who's throwing Jane the you-have-food-in-your-teeth look, and I can only feel slightly better until I look at the screaming steel beast that is The Scrambler, a ride made to mimic the action of egg beaters if the chef was constantly spinning to survey the kitchen, and I think that plus the heat, yes, that is a good idea, but Jane wants to end up in Mike's car, and I have to play the faithful sidekick.

We approach the ride and watching the turn before ours almost makes me dizzy enough, but it is hardly leavened by the ride operator giving us a challenging smile, who says are you guys ready to have your gravities smack the wall, and he hasn't washed his hair or face since I'm sure he can't remember, his skin darker than the soil that coats it, except for the bright white scar that looks like stitches on his left hand and may account for his oddly-length fingers, but sure, I'm ready, back at his tooth hole-gapped smile, for my gravity to do whatever. Mike has his arm over Jane and tucked her into his armpit, which causes her to smile so big she looks like she's smelled honeysuckle in a neighbor's new garden, and Bob's hands are both on the metal gate-fencing and props a foot on the lower rung as if he were to kick off backwards into the backstroke, but it's not like he's ignoring me, more like THIS is his way, capital aloof, but I would like the ride operator to stop eyeing Jane like he's inspired and eyeing me like I'm an option. We each take seats in our individual booths, and Jane's in front of us turning back super excited, and Mike laughs and with a big face says Woah and pulls Jane against him like his gravity's been smacked against the wall even though the ride's not moving, but more so that he can grab and pull her into him with his hand on her right breast. It occurs to me, is this only an opportunity for them to try and get fresh? Bob does have an arm over me, but appears content to leave the friskiness to others. I bunch a fold of my skirt underneath my legs; last thing I need is to be mercy-locked onto the safety bar and then have to pull a hand off of it, ride still in full swing, to stop the free show for the boys waiting in line. There is a buzzer like we should drop under our desks and the ride begins.

You focus on the cart in front of you, but even its minute swaying, reminding you how tenuous the supports are, brings you back to the spinning of everything outside of the ride: the way the colors of everything become reduced to dabs and streaks of pigment, and the elongated stretching. What is particularly odd, is the moment you focus on a single scene, say three elementary school boys in line in front of an overweight woman pulling cotton candy off of her tuft for her adolescent son and the spinning swings in the background, this scene captured in a freeze—the revolution continues, the whole image becomes smaller as you move away, and your neck becomes so craned while trying to parse the colors. It's the neck movement, the wobbling like an overweight candy apple that causes the nausea. Then the cramp in your stomach begins expanding simultaneously to a strange weight in your chest that seems to pull your throat back down to your stomach.

Jane's screaming is a constant siren that attempts to drown out every other sound, and I get to the point where all I can do is push my face into Bob's chest and neck. I'm sure he had no idea what to do, but maybe bat at my shoulder with his palm lightly. I can feel in my chest that it would be a lot better if I could muster the strength to turn my head forward again, but the thought of looking into the spinning again...and I begin throwing up onto Bob's shirt. I can tell he is aware of the vomit when his torso squirms and his legs kick like an infant's, but there's nowhere he can go. And the spinning unites us and pulls us together, and my throw-up unites us both in nausea and the acrid smell, the hot California sun shining on a two-bit ride thrown up days before as part of the county fair, huckstering residents for two weeks a city and then dusty footprints, tire tracks, and crushed paper dishware.

The intensity and wrenching of my stomach that sets my whole body on fire leads directly into the cool and soft exhale and relief of post-sickness. I flush the toilet in front of my face and walk to the bathroom sink to wash my face and wet my neck. I look old today with my eyes pouching fatigue in grey sacks, my cheeks dry and appearing like loose sand, my lips split and dried like expensive sausage. My hair is so thin and without conviction, feels like air when I run my fingers through it. The cool water feels good against my face again, but the mask is the same so I step away from the mirror.

Back in the bedroom the sun highlights the wooden shutters, and the gold of the light gives way to a slotted view of the street when I pull the shutter vents wide. The morning-bright blue sky is cloudless and brilliant over the block where houses still shadow the newly asphalted street, and half of the garbage cans are green in the sunlight and the rest are grey in the shadows, only one comrade having fallen in this morning's collection.

# BLAKE (DECEMBER 10, 2005)

At the Urban Lounge I nurse a stein of beer. I have three dollars in my pocket so this stein represents the night's total indulgence. Nate comes back from the bar with a full stein and two kamikazes in his other hand.

"You want one of these?" he asks.

"No. Thanks, though." I can't start accepting charity now. It will never stop.

On stage is a gothic band making a lot of noise. They have a lead singer and a bassist. A third guy makes the drums and a lot of feedback come out of his laptop. It sounds miserable. Appropriately, the bar is slow this evening. Most everyone at the tables around the dance floor appear to be personal friends or girlfriends of the band members.

"You write today?" asks Nate.

"I'm having trouble starting," I say.

"Will you just man-up and do something?" he says.

"I am doing something: I'm struggling," I say.

Nate sits back in his seat. He doesn't have to say what I know he doesn't want to say again. We've been through this. Instead, he leans forward and says, "I tried something new today."

It's beginning to wear on me to hear about his writing EVERY day, but I humor him. "What'd you do?" I ask.

"Straight drama. Although, it was more like melodrama. I'm not really proficient at the whole straight narrative thing, so I think my shit sounds heavy-handed. It is all about a break-up. No offense. Not like a break-up though, where the characters are pissed off at each other, but basically the girl, Monica, gets a job offer in another state, and her boyfriend, Mitch, is afraid to leave his hometown."

"That kind of sounds like *Good Will Hunting*."

"Yeah, wait. Oww. I guess so, but the premise is not what I was writing. I wrote the one scene. The build-up was unnecessary anyway, because you can figure all of that out by the dialogue." Nate drinks one of his kamikazes. "So they're out to a really nice dinner, sort of a farewell thing. And Monica is begging Mitch to move away. They live in Oregon in a small town that used to have a paper goods factory. Now the town is a dive. Everyone in the town used to work at the factory at one point. So Mitch's parents and all of his friends' parents used to work at this place, until it was shut down in the Mid-80's. Then all of the people started going broke and all of the kids Mitch's age grew up watching their parents' lives collapse. They were like suicide kids in that aspect, because all of their parents were in slow motion downward spirals. And Mitch and his buddies were, like, some of the first kids to munch Oxycotins. I mean hard lives, but not like skid row. Just steadily declining. It's like when I was on the Expos in T-Ball, and we used to lose every game and by about the fourth inning you could always tell it was bad news, because we hadn't scored and the other team would have three runs."

"You didn't use a personal anecdote as a metaphor did you?"

"No. I'm *telling* you that. You get the failure I'm talking about. So Mitch is raised in failure. But he's not a regrettable guy. He just doesn't want to leave all of his friends and his brothers and his parents. At one point or another, he's had to really lean on all of these people. Monica has this great opportunity, only it's in this little suburb of San Diego. She wants Mitch to go with her."

"This isn't like *Menace II Society?*"

"Would you just listen? Damn. *Menace II Society*...you're ruining my story."

"Sorry."

"It gets good. We're getting to the good stuff. Damn." Nate drinks his other kamikaze and then takes a sip from his stein. "So anyway, they're at the fancy dinner. Monica is frustrated, and Mitch is indignant even though he kind of knows that any change might be a really good move on his part. About halfway through dinner, after Monica has almost started to breakdown and cry—she does that half tear thing, Mitch starts to feel bad and humors her. Instead of saying, 'No way,' he starts saying, 'We'll see. It probably is a good idea. I don't know if I can leave, but maybe.' They're starting to get along a lot better, because he humors her with what she wants to hear, and she allows herself to complement his delusions. After dinner they go for a long drive out to the coast and cruise up and down the coastline watching the moonlight shimmer on the ocean. Monica thinks about the fact that in a month she could be staring at the same ocean, but from a thousand miles away in San Diego—"

"*An American Tail?*"

"Ugh...enough. But they park on this one bluff and

overlook the ocean. Naturally, they get down. But the clincher is, and this is the good part, when they're having unprotected sex, Mitch keeps it in when he blows his load because...he wants to leave it up to God to decide."

Nate sits back and takes a satisfied drink from his stein. "You get it, right?"

"Yeah, I get it," I say.

"It's brilliant."

"That sounds...simply amazing."

"You should be amazed," he says. "I'm reaching a new stage of artistic development."

# ALBERT (DECEMBER 17, 2005)

Cardboard boxes fill the basement living room, where my son Blake has moved back, and I sit in front of the television set on a loveseat that used to be one of the front pieces in the family room of our old house. I cheer the television waving my arms in ecstasy. Sometimes I move up into a coiled spring and after a moment, either burst with a grander cheer or sulk in disappointment. I crouch now when behind me and to the right, Taylor comes bounding down the basement stairs. I have to turn most of the way around to see him from the grey and fraying loveseat. For twenty-two his hairline has receded back further than mine, and he keeps his hair cut short. Physically, he is built like I am, heavy in the center. He stands there for a minute moving his mouth, and I click a button on my remote control. After a moment, Taylor looks at me and then looks at Blake's things. Instead of going into his bedroom, Taylor stands by the door as if thinking about something and then heads back upstairs.

With Taylor absent, I pick up the remote control again and continue watching television. After a moment I pause with my head cocked toward the doorway to the basement stairs. Then I stand, click a button on the remote control and walk up the stairs. In front of a steaming oven, Taylor shakes a spice over a pan cooking on one of the burners. He batters the mix around with a wooden spoon and then shakes in a different spice. He pauses with the spice over the pan and then furiously shakes it again. He stirs this again and lifts a spoonful up in front of his face. With his other hand he pokes at the mix and licks his finger. He licks his tongue back and forth across his lips and looks up while deciding on the taste. When he notices me in the doorway he looks over, blinks several times and then turns back to his pan. Within a moment he is back pouring spices in this and chopping up that.

I walk into the great room and drop onto the couch. I pick up the remote control and click it. Behind me Taylor turns around every now and then moving his mouth. After ten minutes, Taylor finally walks into the great room and puts his open hand up next to his wide mouth, while looking up the stairs. He walks back into the kitchen. A minute passes and then Blake comes down from my computer in the office. He pauses halfway down the flight of stairs and looks at me with a heavily somber face and very dark, swampy eyes. His hair is long and mussed. He continues downstairs and heads into the kitchen. Behind me, Blake clears the table. When he has laid out the silverware he walks over to the couch and stands next to me, enraptured by the television, but then walks over to the flight of stairs with his open hand by his wide mouth.

Three minutes pass in which I do not move from the couch, though Blake sets the dishware and glasses on the table, and Taylor organizes the kitchen island into a taco ingredient buffet. Karen makes her way downstairs. I look up from the couch to match her dark, swampy eyes and notice the sleep lines still creased in her cheeks. She wears the same sweat suit she has worn all week. She walks into the kitchen and turns her head back and forth. She looks to the fridge, and Blake with a frustrated posture points to the gallon of one percent milk sitting in the middle of the table.

Karen stands over the kitchen island and directs her attention to me. Looking up to the ceiling, I click the remote control and then join everyone in the kitchen. Karen hovers over the various porcelain bowls. She frowns at the shredded cheese and when she looks at the sliced tomatoes she holds a hand towards Taylor with her thumb and pointer finger extended. She contracts the distance between the thumb and her finger, which causes Blake to look at Taylor and Taylor to turn away from her and walk to the table where he picks up his plate. He comes back to the island and after placing a taco shell on his plate begins to fill in the necessary ingredients. Blake follows in kind and I follow Blake. I am walking to my seat at the dinner table when Karen finally walks over to pick up her plate.

There is a pause at the dinner table while I look at my plate and then to Blake and then to Taylor. And Blake and Taylor look at each other and up at Karen who keeps moving her mouth the entire time she struggles with the various spoons and bowls constructing her taco. Blake reaches down to his plate and picks up his taco to take a large bite. This action speeds up Karen's construction, who rushes to the table and angrily glares at Blake. Karen raises her right hand to her forehead, to her breast, and then both of her shoulders. We reluctantly do the same, until all of us hold our graceful palms together pointed at the ceiling. We finish together, again with our right hands to head, breast, and shoulders.

After a bite of taco, I look to my left at Blake. His chewing is erratic, and, almost imperceptibly, he sways left to right. I point toward his glasses and then at my own. He shrugs. I rub my chin and point to his dark bristles, and he just stares at me. I point at the couch and the television and back to him and then upstairs toward my office. He stares across the table at Taylor's food. At this point Karen begins opening and closing her mouth between mastication. The distant look in her eyes plus her jaw movements remind me of how a horse chews. Taylor does not struggle with chewing. Blake glares back at Karen and then closes his mouth in a snide smile. Karen's face flushes, and she tries to look Blake right in the eye while she dramatically points her fork toward the front door. She huffs and bangs her hand with the fork in it back on the table. Blake looks stony-faced back at Taylor's food.

Everyone chews his or her food.

Slowly, Taylor begins drawing our attention between bites of food. He lifts his right hand up to a great height and then wags it back and forth, back and forth. After another bite of food, he rolls his head around his shoulders and wipes his brow. In a response to Blake, he shrugs and takes another bite of his taco. Blake moves his mouth again, and Taylor, staring at his food, shrugs and then holds up one finger. Again he indicates a height with his right hand, but this time he follows it with both arms extending to a much greater width. Taylor dismisses himself with a wave of his hand and then stares at his plate. There is a concentration in the way he stares at the food on his plate. He picks up a fork and nudges some of the meat and lettuce that have fallen from his taco.

Blake stares off into the distance of Taylor's plate of food watching the fork movement. Blake continues chewing his food and taking fresh bites from his taco, oblivious to the parts falling to his plate. Karen keeps taking bites, but stares into a place between the two somehow managing not to see me in front of her. Although I have no problems staring or chewing, I destroy the formation that was my taco and physically rearrange it. I throw an arm in front of my work and when the others begin to notice what I am doing, I hold up a single finger without hesitating. A few last movements seal my work, and I turn my plate around so that they may notice my taco face. The pieces of lettuce teeth sitting on top of the half taco-shell smile do not line up correctly, but I smile as I point to the tomato eyes and lettuce nose. I then wave my hand over the crushed taco-shell pieces and meat that make up the face's hair.

Blake and Taylor share blank expressions, Blake turning back to stare at Taylor's plate, and Karen outright frowns across the table.

I turn the smile back toward me and mix everything into a taco salad with my fork. Blake stands first after finishing his food and starts making a second taco. Karen waves her arm towards him and the fridge, causing Blake to stop what he's doing and over-exaggerate a sigh. He walks to the cupboard, takes out a glass, fills it with water, and brings it to her. After handing her the glass he bows very deeply which she ignores. Blake finishes making a taco and returns to the table. Over the course of both Taylor and my making new tacos, Karen begins moving her mouth and flicking her wrists. As the momentum of her movement continues, her actions become larger and more exaggerated. Taylor watches her attentively. Blake manages to glance up every few moments. Then Karen pauses. Still looking off to a space above her and to the right, she furrows her brow and puts her arms down. She keeps looking up to the ceiling, while the rest of us continue eating.

Blake is the first one to finish. He wipes his mouth off with his napkin and throws it on his plate. He takes his plate, silverware, and glass to the sink and busses all of them before placing them in the dishwasher. Karen moves her mouth in his direction, and he stops before walking off. His dark eyes open wide and he throws his arm in her direction palm up, while shrugging his shoulders. Karen ignores him and stares straight ahead. Before too much excitement I wave my arms in front of me and point to him and Taylor and me, and then I stand up and bring my dirty dishes to the sink.

Blake and I begin covering the bowls that contain the taco ingredients and placing them in the fridge. Taylor soon stands and after bussing his dishes, empties the leftover meat into a Tupperware container and places that in the fridge as well. Karen, alone at the table, eventually stands and then walks back upstairs without any notice from us. Taylor busses her dishes.

# KAREN (MARCH 14, 1986)

Backing out of Al's childhood home, the tiny house still stupidly smiling: garage for mouth, two windows for eyes, the way it stupidly smiled just after it was built after the end of the last great war, home to the worn husk of a soldier who found comfort and stability in a maternal shrew, someone who wouldn't require him to have to speak anymore. The thin strips of lawn are dry and the green of life has greyed, but I'm sure that's more the effect of never seeing the sunlight on the hazy side of the San Francisco peninsula. The small flowerboxes capping the grass strips against the side of the house are empty after I joked to Dorothy that the plant growing out of one of them looked like marijuana. Perhaps that was the first yard work she had attended to personally in some time. I imagine her, the morning after we left, coming down the stairway from the front door wearing garden gloves with twenty-year-old soil stains and ripping the plant up by its stem. I don't know; it might have been a fern.

But it's good to get the kids to their grandma's a few

times a year, a sense of family. Dorothy has always been good with children, had a few more problems with adults: I let slip a stray comment and no phone call for months. When I hassle Al: we just don't talk that way in my family...things aren't discussed, but I hardly see him flapping jaw in our family either. Assuming he's home from work, and if I'm driving all the way across the bay to drop the kids off and trying to beat evening traffic on the way back, just so the two of us can drive all the way back together: he damn well better be home from work.

The sky is always white and sunless here, the buildings are grey, the grass is grey, and the trees are dark grey. There is almost a total lack of color, aside from a heroic flower blossom or two reaching from a stray box or patch, and, even then, the flowers look too young to have had their color drained out of them. How could I naturally expect any more from Albert than grey? This is what he knows. He used to go to that grey elementary school with the cloudy glass in the windows. He used to caddy at that dull golf course with the black trees. What does he expect of me? My childhood was the color of paper. I remember holding a sheet up to the wall and laughing with Connie after Aunt Margaret wouldn't let us put posters on the wall. We lived in blank paper walls, in a blank paper house. And even that was better than living with my grandma.

After Mom fell sick, but before Dad left, when he still used to go to work, and Mom was in a sedated sleep all the time and always asking things Cindy and I could never have been able to provide. If I say one thing, not even taking into consideration, the soccer teams I sliced oranges and baked cupcakes for, or the volunteering with the reading programs: these kids are spoiled over. At their age Cindy and I used to have to run through the front door, because Grandma liked to hide behind the corner with a belt and whip us, her left hand clutching the small bottle of Jameson's and the brogue coming out in her accent. She sounded more Irish when she drank. And the time she fell over when we ran past her.

We stand just off the kitchen, screams erupting down the hall, and I turn to Cindy who's older, what do we do? Cindy grabs my hand and yanks me out the back door as Grandma scrambles to her feet, and I'm just wishing Mom would hear all of this and wake up. Outside it's sunny and quiet like afternoons can sometimes be, but the intrusion of Grandma's hollering filters through the thin walls, and Cindy's longer legs drag me behind her around the back and along the side of the house, but we duck when crossing the windows in case Gran is still inside looking out of them, and instead of running back in front, we run down the street and then cut into the trees by the creek, and I'm crying and asking Cindy what we're going to do, and she says wait. Can we call Papa? No, you want to sneak back home to call him? We'll stay here until we see his car drive past and then we'll run home.

The water was low in the creek, and I never saw fish in it. We used to hop across rocks or walk across fallen trees, but you had to be careful of slippery moss. One misstep and you could slip your whole foot into the water and ruin your socks. Clomp all the way home leaving wet footprints on the carpet, the grey and stained carpet that everyone always fretted over. Gran could stress and pinch your shoulder while you're sitting with Mom so that you would have to leave, and she walks you down the hall by the collar and bends you over and forces you down to the soiled footprint in the carpet. Her skeletal hand is holding the back of your head like it's a cantaloupe. What do you

see? What do you see?
I'm sorry, Grandma.

# ALBERT (JANUARY 7, 2006)

The left taillight blinks, and a Toyota coupe changes into my lane, so I lightly push my foot against the brake pedal, slow the car to where it will safely coast behind the Toyota. Two people sit in the Toyota. The driver turns his head toward the passenger. Half a block up in the lane to my right, a Jeep accelerates ahead. I raise my eyebrows. I turn on my right turn signal and check my blind-spots. My car changes lanes steadily, and I notice the passenger in the Toyota aggressively turning his head back and forth. The driver fixates on something to his right and the passenger nods his head up and down. Before I can accelerate much, the Toyota's right taillight begins blinking, and it glides into the lane in front of me once again. I press my palm against my steering wheel, and my brow wrinkles. My mouth rapidly opens wide.

There are other cars in the lanes. I look at my car's stereo and press the buttons. My brow slightly wrinkles. I press the buttons again. Without a smile I begin opening my mouth consistently. My eyebrows rise and fall depending on how my mouth opens. And then I pause, look quickly at my radio and wrinkle my left cheek. There are a lot of cars on the road. The sun is low and to my right. I can almost see it out my passenger window. The air is still cool, and, although the sun is bright, the light is flat and pale.

I look at the burger stop as I drive by. The drive-thru has three cars lined up behind a little Geo, whose driver leans out the window in front of the menu sign. I can tell his mouth is opening, and he turns back toward others inside his vehicle. The parking lot is mostly full. My nose twitches. On the large painted sign above the burger stop is the heavy outlined, cartoon painting of a cheeseburger, an order of French fries, and a milkshake whose contents rise above the rim of the cup in smooth contours. The milkshake's contents look as thick as ice cream. My windshield glares in the early evening sun. I pick up the cheap plastic sunglasses from my car's center consul, and I set them on my nose. I pass the burger stop.

An Expedition pulls up to my Camry's left side, and then it slowly accelerates ahead. I squeeze my steering wheel tightly and watch the Toyota in front of me. The driver points to the right. The passenger nods his head, and the Toyota slows down. Its taillights do not blink, and the vehicle stays in my lane. The car stalls as if the driver has hit his brake a little harder, but instead of pulling over to the right, the Toyota accelerates slowly. The driver and the passenger look at a street up ahead, and the car approaches the turn at about half of the speed limit. I check my rearview mirror and look over my left shoulder. Too many cars have begun to pass me in the lane to the left and there is no break in traffic. Again, the Toyota slows to make the right turn, and, again, it continues down the street. Up ahead, the streetlight has been glowing go for some time. The walk signal displays the flashing hand. Traffic is lined up four cars deep in both lanes to the right and the left. The Toyota slows again and makes the right turn. I push my foot against the gas pedal, but cannot accelerate enough to make it through the intersection.

My jaw is clenched so I open my mouth wide and stretch my cheeks. I press the buttons on the car stereo. I stare forward. I glance at the watch face on my left wrist. I look in front of me at the passing cars, but do not focus on any of the particular drivers. To my right across the street is a three-story brick office building with the words, "Gheller Associates," in large brass lettering across the top. I cannot make anyone out through the large, tinted glass entrance. The light changes, and I can accelerate my car.

# BLAKE (JANUARY 7, 2006)

I lie on my bed striped by the dull sunlight that comes down the window well and through the blinds when my cell phone flicks on and starts playing this techno tune that the guy at the store changed to my preset when I bought the phone. I reach to the end table next to my head and pick up the phone, and all it tells me is Nate is calling, but it won't tell me what time it is.

"What up, bro?"

"Were you sleeping?" he asks.

"No. What time is it?"

"Good man. Charly and I are going to be over to pick you up in a half hour."

"What?" I roll onto my side. "No, I got to go look for a job this afternoon." The room is cluttered with opened and half-full moving boxes. Trails run through the boxes: one from the stairway door leads to my old room where my brother sleeps now. The trail branches to the bathroom and to the couch and over to my bed against the wall under the window.

"You don't need to look for a job. You live with your

parents now."

"Well, if I ever want to move out...."

"It's Saturday. You're not going to find a job on a Saturday. You can spare to be broke another day or two. We're on our way. Deal," he says.

Click.

I flip my phone shut and hold the back of my hand with the phone against my forehead like a debutante discovering that the South was lost. I'm tired and nauseated, and I don't know why I'm nauseated, because I spent last night watching TV in my room alone in the dark, trying to decide if alcoholics can go nights with no compulsion to drink, and if I am not an alcoholic does that mean I am responsible for all of my recent behavior? My brother came into my room then, and we made uncomfortable eye contact because I was having trouble with the meaningless "What's up."

When I sit upright, I hold still staring at my swollen belly and allow my stomach to stop fluttering while I breathe through my mouth. Settled, I walk across the room and peek through the door that leads to my old bedroom, my brother's new room and see that he is asleep. I close his door and walk into the bathroom. In the mirror, my complexion looks like soft-mashed potatoes with black olives for eyes. I'm all squints and wrinkles. My skin has grown loose over my muscles.

I take a long shower letting my mind go while soaping and shampooing continuously so as not to forget. The bathroom is cloudy when I step out of the shower, and my skin reflects pink in the mirror. My eyes are softer, and I'm still thirsty, but the cut of nausea has waned. Back in my room I'm dressing when my cell phone rings.

Nate.

"Wear hiking boots, asshole."

"What? No, I'm not—"

"And a jacket, it's cold."

The phone clicks off, and I look at it, but don't call him back. Instead I grab my camouflage pants, hiking boots, and a hooded sweatshirt. I don't argue; I don't think. Hiking boots? I put on hiking boots. Hoodie? I put on a hoodie. My brother is still asleep. The basement is cold, but he is under one of the thick comforters our aunt and grandma made for us when we were kids. His comforter is yellow, and mine is red. I need coffee.

When I open the front door the sky is the color of a dry-erase board and the light is flat. Nate stands at the end of the porchway, the alcove cropping him into the front door picture, making it look like this is the cover shot to Nate's breakout album, and somewhere in the mid-west, a slightly overweight girl with skunk-highlights chopped a-line and in ripped denim jeans and a punk t-shirt is tracing her multi-colored fingernails over Nate's profile while lying on the carpet in her bedroom.

"Why am I outside in the morning?"

"Don't worry, it's going to be awesome." He is smiling as he turns and walks out to Charly's Bronco. It is a genuine smile, and something tickles me thinking about how funny the word awesome is, and how well he delivered that line with no pretense, and for the first time in a little while I think, "This is a beautiful moment." I think about myself thinking this. My friends surprised me in the morning with something to do, and it's different and new, and I don't even know what it is, but I don't think I care.

In the Bronco I sit in the backseat and ask if we can stop somewhere for something to eat or coffee. Nate turns back to me and hands me a thermos with coffee in it, and when I protest that I can just go buy one he says,

"No, that's your coffee. Ours are up here." They made a thermos for me. And, again, this morning is beautiful. I sit back and buzz while the landscape flies by at highway speed. We trace the foot of the Rocky Mountains.

After a few minutes Nate takes a CD out of the book Charly keeps under the passenger seat and slides it into the player. He turns the volume up.

I close my eyes, screaming the words and remember the first beer I ever drank with Nate when we were playing in the arroyo. He told me to pound the beer, and it would taste like Coke. I remember the nights we would stay up almost until morning drinking gin from the bottle and talking about music and literature and how we were going to make it. How it was in the cards, and we were so ready for it. I remember running college workshops with Nate, and how everything we wrote was so much more vital and so much more heroic than everyone else's. I remember when Hyrum asked me why I didn't want to be a doctor or something like that if I was so smart. I remember how Leonardo DiCaprio in *The Basketball Diaries* changed my life.

And I'm in my mid-twenties in the backseat of my friend's SUV driving away from my parents' house, and all around my peers put on their ties to go to work and have business cards. In a few years they will have careers and many already have families. Worse than that are the writers under twenty-five with exciting second novels, and journalists scraping the far sides of the earth.

I try to imagine a way for life to be beautiful in my head that doesn't involve me visualizing a movie montage or a close-up of my smiling face as the camera slowly pulls out. How much of my mind do I control?

We have been driving for forty-five minutes when I

ask Nate and Charly where we are going, and they try to assure me, "Don't worry about it." And it's not that I particularly care, these excursions have become a bit habitual: today we're going to shoot guns, today we're repelling down cliffs, today we're swimming underwater and trying to use plastic bags as makeshift air tanks. It's a bit Soldier-of-Fortune for my taste, but it's more entertaining than the alternative nothing I could be doing.

Nate exits the highway, and we begin driving up a canyon. It dawns on me, "We're heading to your parents' cabin, huh?" I ask Nate.

"Near there, but not quite," he says.

"I don't want to have to shoot or gut anything."

"Don't be a sissy," says Charly.

"It's not like that," says Nate. "I told you, we're hiking."

I'm pretty sure he never said we're going hiking, but I can live with the answer for now. The brisk air flowing down the canyon smells fresh in that way that only cold air can smell fresh. The mountains are mostly covered in snow, but when I mention this to Charly and Nate, Charly tells me to shut up. I'm tired of bitching, and as far as I'm concerned, fuck it, what do I have to lose? More and more I wonder if this is all elaborate penance for the squandering of my last few months.

When we crest the canyon, Charly forks to the left and we begin heading North again around the upper-lip line of a bowl whose base holds what appears to be either a very tiny lake or a very large pond. Traffic infrequently passes and there are no other cars in front or behind us. Charly slows when we reach an unmarked dirt road that leads into the mountains and the trees. What I first mistook for a driveway to a cabin must serve some other purpose as I see neither cabin nor dwelling after several minutes of driving.

"Does someone live back here?" I ask. They ignore me.

Charly drives on, and I can no longer see anything in either direction except for trees and snow. When the car comes to a clearing, Charly shuts the engine off and parks. We leave the car and walk across the clearing, stopping at a single steel pole about waist high and five inches in diameter coming straight up from the snow. Nate pulls his backpack off of his shoulders and unzips it. He hands me a compass and then takes one out for himself.

"Have you ever used one before? It's easy. You line up the red side of the needle on North and then you move it over to whatever degree you want to head to. Once you line the arrow up you pick something out not too far in the distance and you line up to that. You walk over to it, and you do it again. Pretty basic."

"Technically North is not magnetic north," says Charly.

"But we've ignored that when figuring our degrees," says Nate. "If you follow the compass eighteen degrees off of North for about a mile you will come to a small lake. I'm going to go first. Fifteen minutes after I leave, you can take off, and then Charly will follow."

"I'm not going to do that. There's no trail, and I've never done this before. What if I get lost?"

"Go slowly and you'll be fine. It's easy, plus Charly will be behind you to make sure you don't get lost."

I can see our three breaths wafting out of our mouths like escapee souls. Charly has his hands in his pockets and appears bored. Nate looks at me with a sincerity I begrudgingly accept, and he pats me on the arm to acknowledge it. He steps against the steel pole and lines up his compass. He looks into the trees, and then turns to me and says, "Remember, fifteen minutes." Nate walks forward into the line of trees. He reaches one of the trees, touches it with his right hand like he doesn't believe it is really there, and then walks around it. He adjusts his compass again and then walks beyond where I can see. I look at Charly, and he looks at his watch.

"There's no way I'm going to go and get lost in the woods. There's not even a road to where we are that I could get lost and come back to."

"It's really pretty easy. You basically follow a little valley all the way there." Charly has a deceptive smile on his face, his eyes keep secrets.

I look in front of us and can tell by the peaks that there can't be a valley or even a canyon. "No, there's not. The mountains don't do that, do they?"

"No," he says laughing. "You need to use the compass, and you're going to go up and down hills. On the plus side, you don't have to do any climbing."

"Well, I guess that's peachy."

If the hike is only a mile, and I can walk a mile in ten minutes this has to be, what? A thirty-five minute hike, tops? Nate's not an idiot, he would have made me carry water if I needed it. A few more minutes pass, and then Charly says he needs to go grab his bag.

He jumps in the Bronco while I'm staring off into the trees. By the time I run over to where the SUV was parked, his tires spin over the snow, and he disappears down the path. I stand at the edge of the clearing, the sound of the car's engine fading into the silence of the snow. When I was little and learning how to swim, my instructors would goad me into swimming out to them away from the safety of the pool's edge. Once I started swimming toward them, they would walk backward so that I would have to swim farther and farther. Charly just tricked me off of the edge.

I walk back to the steel post in the clearing's center. I set the compass on top of the post and line a tree up with eighteen degrees off of North. The tree has a ruddy knot on it that looks like a winked eye. I walk.

# ALBERT (JANUARY 8, 2006)

I slowly trace a finger along the heel edge of the leather shoe. A young salesman in an ill-fitting suit approaches. He smiles widely. I pick up the shoe and show it to him. He nods his head and backs a step, pivots, and walks away. I look at the shoe from different angles and then set it down. On the other side of the shoe-laden tables are chairs with leather seats and backs.

Across from me, a four-year old boy pulls his left knee up to his chest and tucks his face against it. He frowns his brow and curves his mouth down while the woman next to him places a hand on his back and leans close to his ear. There is another young man in a suit in front of this boy holding a shoe fully-laced but spread open in his hands. The boy shakes his head against his knee. The woman backs up now; the scowl on her face is sharp and angry. The boy slaps his hands onto the armrests and puts his leg back down. The young man, kneeling on one knee while seated over a stool, grasps the boy's foot and fits it inside of the shoe. There is a moment of struggle between the boy and the young man, the foot shakes back and forth while the young man wrestles with the laces. It is secured to the boy's foot, and the boy jumps out of the chair and takes a few steps exaggerating his step into the shoe.

The salesman returns with two boxes of the same shoe I held up for him. His smile full of teeth, he opens the shoebox and pulls the shoe from some tissue paper. He squats in front of me on a stool that has a slanted mirror. I take the shoe and watch his lips move. I stick my foot into the mouth of the shoe and then put my foot on the ground. I lean over my foot and look at it from two angles. The clerk moves his mouth. I nod my head and move my mouth. I stand.

Across from me the boy slumps back into his chair and kicks his shoe off using his other foot. He pulls his legs up to his chest and buries his face between his knees. His mother ignores him and points her finger to the shoes and their box. The young man gathers the items together, and they move toward the register.

I walk six steps in one direction and then seven steps in the other. I look down at my shoes, and I look at the reflection of my shoes in the mirror. My shoes and their reflection.

# ALBERT (JANUARY 9, 2006)

Above the doorway is a sign with two large wood cutouts
of Italian chefs mechanically rotating back-and-forth. The
chef to the right has a black moustache and a little tuft of
black hair coming out of the back of his chef's cap. His
legs are split mid-stride, and he carries a large bowl of
spaghetti in his fingertips. The chef to the left looks
exactly the same except his moustache and tuft of hair are
grey. His legs are split mid-stride, and he carries a large
knife in his right hand and a fork in his left. Directly
below the two chefs, and not rotating, the words
"Donatello and Sons" glow in neon cursive writing. Blake
steps to the front door, swings it open with his right
hand, and walks inside in front of his brother and mother.
Taylor catches the door, but holds it so Karen can step
inside. I take the door from Taylor.

Blake stands in front of the hostess's podium with his
mouth opening and closing. The hostess, young in her
twenties, turns to the right over her shoulder and surveys
an out-of-view section of the restaurant. Several groups
stand in the entryway of the restaurant, but appear to

have more members in their parties than the four of us. The hostess turns back to Blake, nods her head, and her mouth moves. Blake walks back over to the three of us, and Taylor's mouth moves. Blake shrugs his shoulders and shakes his head back and forth quickly while crinkling his nose. To the right of the entryway is the restaurant bar. On one of the television screens plays some basketball highlights. A large player on the Knicks drives to the hoop and slams the ball. I look at Blake and Taylor who stand next to each other, but angled in such a way that they slightly face each other. Taylor's head bobs with excitement while his mouth moves rapidly. Blake smiles, and even Karen is watching Taylor intently. Scruff beard hair and moustache whiskers sprout all over Blake's face. His eyes look puffy behind the glasses on his face. Taylor's face is recently shaven, and he wears a polo shirt and khakis. Blake's old t-shirt has small holes forming, and his baggy jeans fray around his sneakers. I catch Karen's eyes going up and down Blake.

The hostess takes the small stack of menus in her hands and knocks them against the podium to straighten them. Her eyes go bright, and her mouth opens. A large family stands from a bench to our left and follows the hostess, who pivots on her heal to take them back into the dining room. We move to the free bench and sit down. Karen nudges my right arm with her left elbow as her mouth begins to move. I move my mouth. She opens her mouth, and her face forms a half-smile that is almost a sneer. I smile. She moves her mouth more and begins to move her hands as well, careful to keep her purse cradled between her elbow and side. I look away from her to scan my surroundings and then turn back to her. I shrug. She shakes her head and continues to keep moving her mouth. I notice her slow blinks while her mouth moves quickly. Her eyes are dark and her complexion slightly too pale.

Blake jabs me with his right elbow and points to the hostess as he stands; the hostess, once again, blinks her bright eyes and smiles. I follow Blake and Taylor with Karen as we walk through the dining room, most of the lighting comes from the table candles. The hostess weaves between a few more tables and brings us to a round table near a window, but some bushes and cars in the parking lot obscure any view. We take our seats, Karen to my right and Taylor to my left. The hostess places menus in front of us and walks away. The menu is a cardstock folder with the printing on a separate page that must be glued to the cardstock. There are no listings for beverages and the decimal places have been left off of the prices.

Blake reaches for the smaller menu in between the little candle bulb and the salt and pepper shakers. My fingertips tighten their grip on the edge of the menu. Taylor leans over to Blake and folds the top corner of the little menu back a bit so that he can peek. I glance at Karen who continues to examine her menu. Taylor points to something on the little menu and Blake slightly shrugs his shoulders. I close my menu and set it down in front of me. My hands fold, fingers crossed over the menu. My mouth opens as I look from Taylor to Blake to Karen. Blake looks up from the little menu; his mouth moves. Taylor continues peeking over the corner and his mouth moves. Karen stares at a different section of her menu. I look from Blake and Taylor back to Karen. To my left, a family of four vibrates at another round table much like ours. The smiles on their faces stretch their mouths and make their cheeks wrinkle. The father is slightly heavy and tan. He wears a polo shirt and his forearms are also dark. His hair has begun to lightly grey along the edges of his hairline. His wife has bright eyes and her hair is a soft even color with no sign of grey. She still has her figure and lightly squeezes her husband's hand. The children are in their teens, an older girl and boy. The girl has light hair like her mother and dresses neatly. The boy's hair is parted and combed, he appears comfortable in his polo shirt and pants that fit. His hands gesture in front of him, bright eyes, and his mouth moves excitedly.

Karen folds her menu and sets it in front of her. The busser brings glasses of water to our table. Karen takes the little menu out of Blake's hands; her mouth doesn't move. I move my mouth. She does not look at me, but moves her mouth. With his elbows on the table, Blake bends his head down into his hands scratches the back of his head with his fingertips. His hair is evenly long, his bangs hang over the top of his glasses and the sides almost cover his ears. He pops his head back up and looks about the table. I pick up my glass of water and sip. Taylor looks to his right and left somewhere behind me and moves his mouth. Blake moves his mouth and nods his head to his right. I turn my head and see a waitress talking to a table across the room.

Karen folds the little menu and places it back in the center of the table. The waitress from across the room sets a basket of bread in the center of our table and begins moving her mouth. She appears to be in her mid-twenties, close to Blake's age. She taps the pen in her right hand against a notepad in her left hand. I look to Karen who begins moving her mouth. She opens her menu and points to a section on the right side and continues moving her mouth. Karen looks back up from her menu to the waitress who finishes noting something on her pad. The waitress turns to Blake, and he begins moving his mouth. To my left, the other family begins vibrating again. The father has his hand lightly set against his wife's upper arm, but he faces the center of the table, his eyes open wide and his mouth moves rapidly. He lifts his other hand up and begins pointing repetitively at his son. Taylor finishes moving his mouth without breaking his look from the waitress, as he deliberately closes his menu. The waitress looks at her notepad the entire time and nods her head. She looks up at me, and we make eye contact. I move my mouth and point to the menu. She collects our menus and walks away.

I look around the restaurant and move my mouth. Karen moves her mouth, and I look at her. Taylor quickly moves his mouth maintaining a half-smile. Karen moves her mouth again, and Blake shakes his head. His forehead is wrinkled. I move my mouth, and this time Blake holds his right hand over the table, palm up, as he moves his mouth. Taylor shrugs as he moves his mouth. Karen shakes her head and moves her mouth. I move my mouth. Karen looks right at me with wide eyes and moves her mouth faster. Her cheeks tighten.

The waitress returns to our table with the drinks. She sets a glass of dark wine in front of Karen, a mixed drink in front of Blake, and sodas in front of Taylor and me. When she walks away, Karen moves her mouth, and Blake immediately follows her by moving his mouth. Karen looks at her wine, picks up the glass, and takes a sip. Blake looks away from Karen, after letting his glare sink in, picks up his own glass, and drains half of it in one pull. Taylor stares at something on the tablecloth in front of him and intently picks at it. I look over to my left with my elbows on the table and my hands folded. I lightly bob my mouth against my folded hands. The other family is consumed by eating their food. I turn back to the center of the table, take my elbows off and set my hands flat in front of me, my mouth moving slowly. Taylor looks up from picking at the tablecloth and looks at me. His mouth moves. Karen swirls the wine in her glass. Taylor looks at all of us at the table individually. Blake puts his elbows on the table, removes his glasses and rubs his eyes.

The waitress brings out our salads and Taylor's bowl of soup. She walks around the table taking turns offering to grind fresh pepper over our food. Taylor leans forward over his soup and softly blows. Before the waitress leaves, Blake points to his drink and holds his finger up in the air. The waitress nods and walks away. I notice Karen look at Blake, but then return her eyes to her salad. I eat salad. Blake jabs his lettuce with his fork. Taylor tears a piece of bread from the bread basket and swirls the corner of it in his soup. Karen eats her salad with delicate little fork strokes. I take a piece of bread from the basket and tear the center of it out. I set the crust of the bread on the bread plate and take bites of the piece in my fingers.

The waitress returns to clear our dishes. She also brings a fresh drink for Blake and refills sodas for Taylor and me. Blake takes a large sip from his drink. His eyes soften. The waitress carries a large tray over her left shoulder and a serving stand in her right hand. She unfolds the stand and sets her tray on top of it. She presents Karen with a plate containing a chicken breast and some pasta and vegetables on the side. Blake receives a large plate of rigatoni in a marinara sauce. She gives Taylor the lasagna and me a plate with veal and pasta. We all take fresh parmesan except Karen. We eat without moving our mouths, and I watch the family to my left stand from the table and leave.

When the waitress comes to our table Blake points to his empty drink, and Karen taps on her wine glass. The waitress returns and replaces the empty glasses. Before taking a drink from his fresh glass, Blake takes a sip of water. Karen drinks from her glass, sets it down, and moves her mouth. Taylor looks at Karen and moves his mouth. I move my mouth and look from Taylor to Karen. Karen looks right at me. I lightly scratch my fingernail on the tablecloth and move my mouth again. Taylor shakes his head and moves his mouth. He looks back and forth between each of us and continues to move his mouth. I shake my hand pointing at his food. He stops moving his mouth and takes a bite of his lasagna. We take bites and chew our food. Occasionally, we bob our heads. A busser has begun to clear the table to my left. He walks away from it with a tub of dirty dishes.

Karen slowly stirs her pasta with her fork. She does not take a bite, but I turn back to Blake and Taylor. In between bites of lasagna, Taylor moves his mouth. Blake lazily bobs his head, but does not look up from his food. Having finished his cocktail, he takes a long drink of water. The busser finishes setting the table to my left. We chew our food and no one stops to move his mouth. I take a forkful of veal and dab it in the sauce. I chew it slowly. The hostess brings a young couple to the table to my left. The boy slides the chair in for the girl when she sits. They both smile showing lots of teeth. The boy leans forward. The girl vibrates. Blake raises his cocktail glass, swirls the ice inside, and brings it to his lips. When the waitress returns, she collects Blake's and my empty plates. She stands next to the table and looks at each of us. Blake and Taylor shake their heads. I hold my hand, palm down, over the table and move it back and forth horizontally. She walks away. I lean back in the chair and run my palms over my chest. I look at Karen, Taylor, and then at Blake.

# TAYLOR (DECEMBER 5, 2005)

I sit in front of the canvas slumped over my stomach. My breath exhales in damp pants that cause my body to feel like drying clay. I look over and notice Carrie staring at me so I shrug to her. I don't slowly straighten my posture until after I'm staring at my canvas again hoping she won't notice my effort to sit upright. Like maybe she'll look at me again and think, there's Taylor with great posture: he's always had great posture.

Off to the side of me, Dr. Johnson tinkers with something sitting at one of the back tables. In front of the class, burning under three sources of light is a mallet, a stuffed cat, a glass ball, and a tattered overcoat. There's classical music playing, maybe Bach, and all of the other students swipe away at their canvasses. They look from their canvases to the objects and then back again, dabbing at their palettes, twirling brush ends, and then daubing the canvas. A mallet, a stuffed cat, a glass ball, and a tattered overcoat—they sound like the ingredients to a television witch's spell. There isn't even harmony in the grouping. Why would a mallet be next to a stuffed cat? A garage tool next to something from a six year-old's bed; it doesn't make any sense. I realize they are contrasting elements, but the grouping is obviously and painfully a pose. It's difficult to accept. I imagine some sarcastic critic saying, "Oh, I love the painting where you obviously put together objects that should never be put together...what will you gather for your next still-life: a snowflake fashioned out of butter, a Raggedy-Anne doll, and hot lava?"

I look at the ground. I'm slouching again. I avoid looking in Carrie's direction. A glass ball, a mallet. I have painted the ground on the canvas: this vibrant, but cool green. Something like a moss color, not bright with the sun, but full of life like shade, like the underside of a rock. There is depth, and it is breathing. I could paint that, because it was an abyss. It didn't ask to be painted, it simply was. Not like a stuffed cat or a tattered overcoat. Everyone turn toward the camera, smile. A glass ball, a stuffed cat, a tattered overcoat....

I'm staring at the mallet when I see the fire, but it's not the mallet on fire, it's the glass ball. The flames lick up the sides of the ball in wavy striations of pigment. The fire makes the ball shimmer.

I put it on my canvas that way by flicking my wrist a little bit. That's it. This tiny flick, and I paint everything else exactly the same. For the mallet I keep everything cold, the glisten exact and sharp. The steel head is a keystone anchoring the entire canvas. Your eyes will be able to tousle the kitty or explore the ball, but when they hit that mallet they will sink. That's why the fire came from the mallet but was in the ball. The light only burns when it's over an abyss. This is the strange contradiction of my rejuvenation: it comes from the dark abyss and not from the light. I don't know why, but all of my life comes hammering against that mallet, decisions and variations drop. The clank, quick-change and I'm painting this mallet and this stuffed cat like I've never seen either object before in my life. Like I have no idea what domestic objects are, like I'm from the clay, from the mud. The glass ball, the tattered overcoat—these are less objects and more shapes. The fire and the mud. But nothing changes in the way I paint. The mix of the colors. I flick my wrist, but I can't see the mallet or the tattered coat. There are edges, and there are folds; the curves connect.

People have begun to start cleaning up. They clean their brushes, wash their hands, breakdown their easels. Dr. Johnson has made his rounds and bid adieu. He packs papers and books into a shoulder bag. I twist-press and pull the layers of the coat. The cloth folds and crevices. The pockets of a bunched coat.

"Wow...you really stepped up," says Carrie over my shoulder. I flinch from her proximity, but keep my eyes on the canvas. My brush down, I allow myself to slouch.

"I still have to figure out the cat," I say without much enthusiasm.

"The coloring is brilliant. Look at that," she points at the ball.

"I get lucky sometimes…. Are you bailing?"

"I'm going to get some food at Ed's before my next class…. You want to come?"

"I'm going to pour a little more hurt on the canvas before I leave." I smile.

"I'll see you Wednesday then."

The mallet and the cat. Carrie looks good. I start dabbing my palette for the cat fur. The classroom is quiet. Martin is on the other side, but concentrating. I have to put the cat between the mallet and the ball.

I leave awhile later, Martin with his headphones on, my canvas close to completion, close to abandonment. Something hit against the mallet this afternoon. This is my theory; it can be my new religion. Life in the colors, the mallet and the ball, my exhales are only breath, and I deserve to slouch. Today I could put my painting away with no desire to destroy it. The afternoon is grey, and the painting is unfinished, but I'll have time tomorrow.

# ALBERT (JANUARY 10, 2006)

I park on the street and put a couple of coins into the parking meter. I look at my watch while walking down the street. The bank is on the first floor of a tall building. I step to the back of a line that zigzags back and forth several times. When I join the line, the lady in front of me with crossed arms twists around, looks at me, and then twists back. She keeps touching the pointer finger of her right hand against her left elbow. Three tellers are working. One teller is in her late thirties; the others are a boy and a girl in their twenties. The oldest teller is heavy-set and has lighter hair that is cut short and parted on the right side. She wears a generic cotton dress. The male teller wears a tie but no jacket. His hair is spiky. The younger female wears a well-fitting pantsuit and has bright hair cut chin-length. Freckles speckle her cheek bones.

The woman in front of me half-twists toward me with her arms crossed, reaches up to her head with her right hand and scratches it with her index finger, raises her eyebrows, and then half-twists away. I stare at the floor.

The pattern of the tile, a combination of granite slate and polished marble, looks like x's when I turn my head one direction, or like crosses when I turn my head the other. The rectangle counts create an equation of four five-squared edges of slate to create a square space filled with sixteen smaller marble tiles. The relationship ties together in the pattern's twenty slate squares to its sixteen marble, or the four more that make the five by four twenty. It seems simple until I literally count the slate tiles in one pattern and discover that there are sixteen squares and not twenty. The literal count brings another type of balance to the pattern, but this time there is the tension of two equalities struggling for size: one swallowing the other.

The younger tellers push through their customers faster than the older teller. The woman in front of me has begun to wave her hand in front of her face. Her mouth is slightly open, and she sways right and then left. When it is her turn, the older teller looks at her and the lady steps over to the counter. And then the male teller finishes serving a Latino customer wearing dirty jeans and a t-shirt. He smiles when I approach the counter. His teeth are straight. His mouth moves and mine moves in response. I slide some cash and papers across the counter. He takes the items and separates them into piles. He feeds the cash into a machine and runs some papers into another machine. He then places the piles into a drawer and taps a button on his keyboard. This prints a receipt he hands straight across the counter to me. His mouth moves again while he looks me right in the eye. This time I shake my head.

I place the receipt into my wallet, fold the wallet in half, and place it back into my pocket. I walk over the pattern of slate and marble. I walk through the double-set

of swinging glass doors. The sun shines brightly, but with
no hurry.

# ALBERT (JANUARY 11, 2006)

Today: the flickering of panted legs and leather shoes passing my door. At maybe the fifteenth or thirty-eighth person, I stand, walk to my office door, and look down the hallway. For a moment there is no one. Then Dean pops out of his office and slips into the lunch room. In a minute he returns swirling a cup of coffee in his right hand and goes back into his office.

I return to my desk and stare at the chart on my computer screen. The flickering light moves tiny niches up and down tracing larger waves, its dance working its way further and further down to the bottom right of the chart. I lean back in my chair and tap my desk and stand up again. I walk to my doorway and don't see anyone in the hallway. I walk down the hall toward the lunchroom peering into each office as I pass. Everyone is on the telephone: Monica, with the phone tucked under her left ear, nods her head while typing on her computer; Dean holds the phone with his left hand to his left ear and nods his head at spaced intervals. He moves his mouth.

The younger ones in the cubicles are not on the

phones, but all watch different charts on their computer screens. The exact charts are different, but the patterns move in the same direction. In the corner cubicle David turns to me briefly as I pass him.

In the lunchroom I open the cupboard with the Styrofoam cups. I remove a cup from the plastic sleeve and place it on the counter. I return the other cups back to the cupboard. I pour coffee into the cup from a half-empty pot and return the pot to the burner. I take three packets of sugar from the basket, tear the ends off of them, and pour them into the cup and slip a stir into it. I step over to the fridge, pull it open, and remove a plastic bottle. I flip its plastic lid back and pour the half-and-half into my coffee. I drip an extra drop. I pull the fridge back open and return the bottle. I step back to my coffee and stir. I bring the cup to my lips and blow across the surface. I take a sip and lift my eyebrows.

I place the cup back on the counter, clap my hands and rub them together and smile. I pick the coffee cup up and step back into the hallway. As I pass Dean's office he looks up at me with his phone still against his ear. I hold my coffee cup and walk back into my office. I step back around my desk and sit down.

I bring the cup to my lips and blow across the top. I take a sip and set the cup on a saucer to my right. I look at my computer screen and push a button on my keyboard. I move the mouse around the mouse pad and use the right click button. I make several left clicks. I stare at the screen for a minute. I left click the mouse and then read several paragraphs on the screen. I move the mouse again and make more left clicks. Then I put my hands on the keyboard and type for several minutes, watching my words appear on the screen and occasionally looking at the keyboard.

I look up to the door. The words:

`I   hope   you   understand   what   is`
`happening.`

Ed stands in the doorway blocking out almost all of the light from the door. His cheeks pull his big bearded mouth into a grin. He steps into my office. I point to my screen while my mouth moves. I hold my hand out with my palm up. I put my hand down and stop moving my mouth. With his hands folded behind his back, Ed paces to one side of my office, pivots on his heel, and paces back to the other side. He pauses, turns to me, and begins moving his mouth. He holds out his left hand with its palm turned up and begins raising it up and down in a jerky motion. He stops moving his mouth when he rotates his extended hand and slides it to the side in a sweeping stroke.

Briefly I look at my computer screen and, with the index finger on my right hand, scratch the side of my head. I move my mouth while raising my right hand up and down in a chopping motion. I point my hand at the computer screen and then shrug my shoulders. Ed's brow furrows and his bushy eyebrows come together. His pupils fall to the ground and then his head snaps up. His eyes squint tight into a glare and he moves his mouth more and then steps out of my office and is gone.

I prop my chin on my thumbs and rub my temples with my index fingers. I close my eyes and exhale. I lean back in my chair and take a drink from the coffee cup. I swirl the coffee in my mouth before swallowing. I set the coffee cup down and look at the computer screen. I put my hands back on the keyboard and finish typing. After rereading the screen, I put my hand on the mouse and move it around. When I stop moving the mouse I left click it. I tap my index fingers against the wood of my desk and then fold my hands.

In the pencil drawer I slide open with my right hand is the novel that I am reading. I reach for it, but do not pick it up. Instead I remove one of the photographs and set it on my desk. With my right hand I pick up my coffee cup and take another sip. I place the cup back on its saucer. The photograph is from my next door neighbor Julie's fifth birthday. In the picture Julie smiles with a face smudged with vanilla cake frosting and a plastic, crumbful plate in front of her. Her hair is decorated with ribbons in her pigtails.

I look back to my computer screen. I place my hand back on my mouse and move it around. I left click the mouse four times and the chart reappears on the screen. The flickering light continues to move up and down building waves. I look at my photograph again and then place it back in my pencil drawer.

# ALBERT (JANUARY 12, 2006)

The sky is a flat white, the clouds almost evenly blocking the afternoon sun, and a cold wind breaches the half-rolled windows of David's Honda Civic. His right hand pulls away from his mouth with the home-rolled cigarette between his pointer and index finger. He sets his palm against the steering wheel for a moment and then extends the entire arm across his body and flicks the cigarette with his thumb expelling burning ash from the car. David turns to me with his mouth moving, his teeth bright white. He is probably only two or three years older than Blake, but dresses well and although they both share shoulder length hair, David keeps his hair pulled back in a neat ponytail.

His shoulder shrugs, and his right arm waves the glowing cigarette while his mouth moves. I move my mouth and scratch my left knee with my index finger. My eyes scan David's car which is immaculate, no trace of ash even, and the only transgression is a Microeconomics textbook on the rear driver's-side seat. Even his ashtray, which is open so his phone can charge in the cigarette lighter socket, is spotlessly clean. There is no sign that he is a smoker.

David watches the road and intermittently stops moving his mouth to inhale his cigarette. He turns to me and holds the cigarette out to me pinched between his pointer finger and thumb. I hold my left hand palm toward him and shake my head. He smiles, flashing his bright teeth. I shake my head again, but smile. David shrugs his shoulders and takes an inhale while watching the road. Again, he crosses himself and ashes out the window.

Five minutes later we pull into the parking lot with Becky, Dean, and Lindsay already walking toward the entrance. The car windows have already been rolled up, and the cigarette has been flicked out the window. We join the group in the foyer of the restaurant, in front of the hostess's podium. There are eight of us including Ed Morgan. The hostess takes the menus from a stack and leads us through the restaurant to a large round table in the back. Dean sits to my right, and Becky sits to my left. Becky moves her mouth as she sits down, and I smile. Dean turns to his left to face Becky and me and picks up his napkin with his silverware rolled up inside. He moves his mouth while polishing his silverware with the cloth napkin. Becky smiles.

A busser circles the table pouring everyone glasses of water. David, who sits over to my left, runs his left palm over his hair and moves his mouth. Everyone at the table looks at him. He looks around the table randomly, shrugging his shoulders while his mouth is in a moving smile. Lindsay moves her mouth, causing David to turn to his immediate left. David looks at Lindsay and nods his head to the left and right. From across the table Ed Morgan moves his mouth, and everyone turns to him. Ed

Morgan moves his mouth and scratches at a bit of the table cloth with his left pointer finger while looking at all of the people around and across from him. Ed's cheeks pull into an inflated smile while his mouth moves. Dean moves his mouth and unfolds his hand in Ed's direction. Ed's cheeks are still pulled back, but Dean's mouth is straight under his moustache. They look at Charles whose hands are loosely folded and is twirling his thumbs. Charles's round, empty eyes look from one to the other and then slowly scan the rest of us. He vigorously nods his head sending his thin, parted hair into a flapping frenzy. He moves his mouth quickly.

A male waiter, who appears to be thirty with short dark hair, presents himself over David's shoulder to the table. He moves his mouth and circles the table while handing everyone a menu. Having completed the circle he pulls a pen and notepad from his apron and looks about the table. I open my mouth, but Ed Morgan moves his mouth, and the waiter smiles, bows his head, and slips the notepad and pen back into his apron as he turns to walk away. Dean leans slightly toward me and barely moves his mouth at all. My shrug appears more like a shoulder twitch.

Ed Morgan picks his menu off of the table with both hands, pinching the edges, and snaps his elbows to extend the menu in front of him. I angle the menu up slightly with a few fingers of my left hand using my thumb as the fulcrum. Everyone looks at their menus except for David who has leaned heavily on his right elbow, propping his head up with his hand and moving his mouth toward ry. His nails are well-manicured. My own nails are not. Becky leans toward me without taking her eyes off of her menu or tilting her head and moves her mouth. I shrug; I gesture to a section of the menu with my right hand and move my mouth. Becky looks at me behind her large glasses, smiles, and raises her eyebrows.

Finished looking, Ed Morgan sets his menu flat on the table and looks around at everyone. He moves his mouth loosely towards the center of the table to which various mouths open and close without much enthusiasm. Dean turns to Becky and me and moves his mouth. His eyes move back and forth between us and his pupils dilate as his mouth moves faster. His mouth pauses in a smile between breaths. His two hands gesture to a space between them while his mouth moves. I take a sip of water. Across the table Ed moves his mouth. Dean's shoulders cringe, and his fingers tense in front of him. He turns toward Ed, but the waiter appears behind David again and holds his notepad and pen.

Ed moves his mouth while the waiter scribbles on the notepad, the rest of us: our lips held tight.

# BLAKE (JANUARY 16, 2006)

"You know, I think I have forgiven myself for the last few months," I say to Nate across the booth table in the back of the Urban Lounge. When I came in, I was surprised to see that they had reupholstered all of the stools and booths. It's not that the fresh red leather looks out of place, but to see investment in the bar...it was a bit disconcerting.

"Thank God," he says with mock sincerity. "You don't even sound like you're merely rehashing quarter-life crisis stuff." Nate swirls the contents of his kamikaze once and then drinks it. A girl in her twenties with oil-black hair trimmed chin-length with bangs stands up from a table near our booth. We make eye contact before she turns to the bar. Her face looks like it could be on a bag of cookies.

"I don't know what I became, or what I expected, but the beast is dead. I am going to start writing again for the shear pleasure of words. Not for some sort of conquest."

"Exactly. The point is the work. Remember it all started with that? The lost book and muted speech? The apartment, the job, the girl—those are incidentals." I nod my head. "The point was to get back to writing again."

"So was all of this," I wave my hand, "with the hikes and everything, was all of that, like a shock therapy or something?" I ask.

Nate's face changes subtly. The smile stays, but the jocularity fades. "Uh, no," he says. "That's different, but don't worry about that."

I sit back perplexed. The band on stage sets up equipment and tests their instruments. I recognize a few of the members. The black-haired girl from the neighboring table makes her way back from the bar, and we share eyes quickly, a secret.

"What about you? You must have something new going on in the book," I say. I pick up my pint of water and sip tasting the metal of hard water.

"What? That's me," Nate says and kicks his knee up. He sits in a half crouch behind the table. "I gave up on my novel a while ago. Who cares?" Nate pulls a pack of cigarettes from underneath the table and removes one.

"You didn't quit. Your novel is all-encompassing. You could write anything and that would count as part of it."

"Well," Nate says with his lips around a cigarette and his eyes smile at me as he lights the end, "maybe I didn't quit. I mean, I'll never really quit. Why else would we be here, right? I have worked on this one new scene."

I smile. It feels fresh to smile now; like I haven't really smiled in a long time.

"This is one of my favorite new scenes, because the main character begins to slip into madness—"

"Cheers," I say holding my water for a toast. Nate smiles and clinks my glass. We drink.

"It's a woman. The single working mother that has had so much political sway. She works in a warehouse fixing pegs into cuckoo clocks...sort of assembly line work, and her hours are those ridiculous morning hours, from like five or six A.M. until two, that places like warehouses seem to keep."

"I think that's so people can work at places like that and keep second jobs. So they don't expect too much compensation."

"I guess, but she works until two o'clock every day, and then she can come home and be with her eight year-old son, Colin. He's in third grade and gets home from school at about that time every day. And Colin's father is still peripherally around. He's a good guy: always pays child-support and takes Colin on the weekends so Macy, that's her name, can sleep in. Like Macy and the baby-papa just didn't really get along when they lived together, but they don't have animosity towards each other. I really want to, like, show something else with the father, you know?"

"What's his name?"

"The father? I don't know. I may have mentioned 'Cliff' somewhere or something. He hasn't appeared in the scene or anything. He's in the background. The story is really, densely layered that way. It's not one of those thinly-veiled-these-are-all-of-my-friends-and-Johnny-said-this-so-I-wrote-it kind of stories. This is a scene all about textures. What happens isn't all that impressive. She wakes up, and it's Saturday morning, and she's slept in really late for her, which means nine o'clock or something. And she's groggy and waking and still sort of half-asleep. Because she slept for so long, she is tired. And getting up, she goes into the kitchen and makes a cup of coffee. She doesn't have a coffeemaker, so she has this little tin cup...."

# ALBERT (MAY 9, 2006)

I set my suit coat on the lawn to my right and unbutton
my shirt cuffs. With them unbuttoned I push my sleeves
up my forearms. I cross my legs in the grass in front of
me exposing my dress socks. I lean back against the hill
supporting myself on my hands. In front of me, the
manicured lawn of the park runs ahead into an open area.
To the right of the open area on the other side of the
fence sits the high school's track. I can see the track 'n
field team practicing. A coach works with a group of
about ten students on sprint starts. The students take
turns. They crouch on the blocks, the coach raises his gun
in the air, the students raise their hips, smoke comes out
of the gun, and the students spring forward and run ten
yards. Inside the track, one student practices his approach
to the pole vault. He runs down a narrow path carrying
the pole, but does not plant it into the ditch. After he
races by the coach, the coach makes little marks near the
ditch. The boy walks back to where the coach is and
looks at the ground with the coach.

    I stare out across the valley with the sun still high

overhead. A couple of joggers run toward me along the left fence of the park. A boy and a girl—they appear to be in their mid-twenties. The boy glances at me as they jog past, up to the top of the hill and around on the sidewalk. Above me, up on the sidewalk, a lady in her fifties walks her Labrador in the other direction. Intermittent students jog at an even pace around the track. While jogging they occasionally pair up with each other for short stretches, but these couplings soon fade and one leaves the other.

Inside the far bend of the track, some high jumpers work with a coach on their jump approaches. The pit pads and bar have been pulled aside and a group of students take turns running to the line. The coach makes a small mark on the ground at the beginning of the approach. The student puts his front foot on the mark. The coach walks back over to where the bar would be, and then signals the student. The student runs in an exponential curve toward the coach and then passes him. Having watched the student's feet, the coach makes a tiny mark on his clipboard. Each student runs up to the coach two or three times.

A moth lands on my ankle, and I shake it away. My hands itch, so I lean forward and slap the blades of grass off of them. In the park the tree leaves shimmer slowly, but I do not feel a breeze. Behind me a jogger turns off of the sidewalk and passes me down the hill. He continues running along the fence to my left. I lift a plastic bottle of water from the grass next to me and take a drink. I raise my left wrist and look at my watch. I look out over the park, and the sun still hangs in the sky. I pick the front of my shirt with my right hand and shake it a few times.

I watch the high jumpers. They gather in a group around the pads and pull them back into place. Individuals take the bar stands and the bar is mounted.

The group splits into two sections at the beginning of the approaches. There are only three left-footed jumpers. The coach stands off to the side of the pit. The first jumper approaches the bar and clears it easily. Each student takes a turn and warms up. The coach raises the bar and all of the students take turns again. It isn't until two jumps later that the bar is knocked down. By this point the jumpers are starting to push themselves to get over the bar. The different levels of form are starting to show. Two more jumpers knock the bar down at this height. The three jumpers do not get another turn. Once the jumpers knock the bar down they stand off to the side of the pit and watch the rest. When the final jumper clears a height that no one else can make, the other jumpers bounce up and down. The jumper goes back to his mark, and the coach raises the bar. Again the jumper clears the bar, and again he goes back to his mark. He is not concerned with how high the others can jump.

# TAYLOR (JUNE 5, 2006)

I poke the garage door button to raise the mechanical door. The warm sunlight floods the garage washing out the garage's florescent glow, and I inhale the desert's wooden smell. I took over the whole garage when spring semester ended, and I told everyone I wanted to have a big workspace this Summer. The cars, two by two, crowd the driveway.

The garage shades me from direct sunlight, but I still take off my shirt in the ninety-degree heat. I arrange my two easels, attempting to line them up the best I can. Then I turn to the drop-cloth spread across more than half the garage, in which lies the giant canvas I stretched yesterday. I left it canvas-side down to keep dust from collecting on it overnight. I put my foot against the corner and pull it up from the side, which is the only way I am able to pick it up. Once it is vertical, I slide my hands across the top holding it steady until I reach the middle. I raise the canvas a foot off the ground and rotate around so I can baby-step the canvas to the easels.

I have to nudge the canvas different ways to settle it

onto the easels, but they hold. The result is this massive blank space that from my perspective appears limitless. I open a can of gesso and blank all of the canvas's pores with a dull white-wash. When I finish I sit on a folding lawn chair in front of the drying canvas and lean back sucking up Summer.

# KAREN (JUNE 5, 2006)

Luce tells me on the way to the meeting not to expect a panacea, not to look to cure anything, but to be open, to go through the motions, to accept the possibility of a new way of life. She keeps phrasing every sentence so delicately with so many precious pauses that by the time she actually hits a breath, by the point I have given up all hope of ever replying, I'm knocked off-guard by her sudden silence. When I speak, my breath surprisingly fails me like suddenly having an ankle give out, my speech is legless. Yes, I mutter, I…it is time. My throat closes on me, and I turn my face into the passenger window, casting my face toward the blinding sunlight, burning the tears up before I end up with streaked red cheeks. You're fine, says Luce. This is an important step that isn't easy to take, but you must make it every day.

When Luce showed up on Saturday the garage had been open, Taylor working on some painting, but was in the basement at that moment, so rather than keep standing at the front door ringing a bell none of us heard, Luce entered through the garage door calling hello, hello which I could hear from the bedroom, the door open. I don't remember saying anything, but remember something being said, and Luce standing in the doorway of the bedroom with an expression on her face I remember distinctly. It was as if the expression encapsulated a growing issue that becomes a concern that becomes beyond the pretense of even trying to hide the bottles anymore, these glass towers like a mini skyline I must have stared at for hours every day of the last couple of months. Luce's expression took in all of that and said yes-I-understand and, also, I-am-so-sorry with a little hint of I-should-have-been-here-sooner, and because of that expression, I started crying. I don't know how many tears I shed that afternoon, but I could probably assign one to every person I have ever met in my life in every instance I have known them and the number would be close, these tears including I-love-you's to my sister and mother, my father wherever he went, my children wringing them out like pearls from oysters, and then a husband incapable of speaking up.

I told Luce that afternoon that I wanted my life back, that I was willing to take drastic measures, that I don't even know where I existed anymore, that my days were stringing together, and that I wanted set points on the timeline. She held me, the tears she spilled were those in empathy, and whispering in my ear that it will be one of the hardest things I ever do in my life, but it isn't impossible. It just takes patience and time. Tears that will wash.

# ALBERT (JUNE 5, 2006)

I sit at the kitchen table with my hands on the table and my fingers crossed. Blake and Taylor sit across from me. Both of the boys look healthy, but they have blank expressions. Blake trimmed his hair short, and he wears contacts instead of his glasses. Taylor's skin is tan from the time he spends in the garage. We sit there for a minute and Blake turns to Taylor and moves his mouth. Taylor looks at him and then moves his mouth.

Before they start a conversation I say:

"When your mother left today with Luce...I...I should have...the one to help...you can't redo...but you can do things that will help her with addiction but...it is something that maybe I will never understand and what do you say...it is time...there is nothing to say other than yep there is less than a ten percent chance of sobriety or yeah most members quit before two months or...so the statistics the science and analysis won't help...if the members are all assholes or...but maybe passing out and your best-friend finding you in bed soaked in your own urine isn't your bottom and maybe we will all revert back to our old unhealthy ways…as to be expected…but you guys appear…it is time…if I could tell you what I've been wanting to say or…see if I had…to convey the unspoken…but it is this lapse that so often isolates us…that part where words fail us or where we discover we are inarticulate…suppose you never try to say a particular sentence…how do you even know you can say it…maybe I don't know…but I want to talk about you guys and your mother…I want us to help her with this…and I want to talk to you guys…you know you can always…tell me or ask me…anything you want right…I will not…I mean I want you to understand that…oh…how to say it…to say to you that you've come a long…or no that you…I'm proud of you…stop…we have all been through…or no…for the last few months…there have been issues…that we…these issues that you…for the last few…I'm proud of what…ahhhh…to myself…I want you to speak…you kids…I need you to help me help your mother…persist."

## BLAKE (JUNE 5, 2006)

I lie on my bed staring at two people talking on the television. The two people discuss the possibility of love between strangers. They discuss this for over an hour. They worry about the kids they have and the kids they haven't had. They worry about the fate of the fucking world. Where will their careers be? The woman wants an opportunity to make a difference.

Taylor sits on the couch flipping through a graphic novel. He looks up every few minutes.

"What do you think?" I ask.

"It's good. It's very in the moment," he says. He yawns and stretches his arms.

"I like it," I say.

"I'm going to bed. Do you want me to turn off the lights?" he asks. He stands up, stretches again, and turns off the movie.

"No," I say. I roll my legs off the bed. "I have to write before I go to bed."

"Jesus," he says. "You should have done it earlier."

"Whatever. I'll do it now," I say and walk over to my

desk. This night will finish when I say so.

# ABOUT THE AUTHOR

Christopher Patrick Steffen was raised in the Bay Area and Salt Lake City. His first book, *Thank You for Supporting Our Dreams*, was published in 2012. He has held a myriad of retail, service, hospitality, and office jobs. At this moment he may be serving you. He lives in Oakland.